THE TRADE

Trace Evans

The Trade is a work of fiction, written for entertainment. The names, characters, places, and incidents portrayed in the story are either imaginary or have been used fictitiously. Any resemblance to actual persons living or dead, businesses, companies, governments, events, or locales is entirely coincidental.

First Edition

Cover design: Sergio Barrera
Photo Credit (Troodos Mountains): Brawphoties

ISBN: 978-0-692-56414-1

The Trade (Synopsis)

A phenomenal discovery in the most unlikely of places: An international team of geologists finds huge—and hugely valuable—quantities of lithium on the island-nation of Cyprus. Before long, the head geologist is found dead; international delegations from near and far arrive in search of the lithium rights; intelligence agencies monitor the situation from the shadows; and the mysterious Swiss-based multinational CORE sends in its ace deal-closer, Monir Young, to represent the company's interests. CORE's ruthless covert operators have laid the groundwork for Monir to acquire the lithium rights unchallenged. But the purchase talks take a dramatic turn when Monir discovers his employer's role in a sinister hidden agenda. As he scrambles to expose CORE's plans, Monir enters the crosshairs of powerful conspirators whose objective is to use the lithium's enormous financial worth for their own geopolitical advantage—and, ultimately, global control.

CONTENTS

1

THE FIND

September: Cyprus

The rain had left a mess. Stalo had been out on her porch for about an hour, mopping out the last section of her house's marble veranda floor, when the small convoy of SUVs drove by. Three Toyota RAV4s. Four people in the first two cars, and three in the last. Red license plates—the most distinguishing mark of rental cars in Cyprus.

The driver of the front car waved. Stalo looked up and nodded. A faint smile formed on the right side of her face.

Davin and his scientists. They must be heading back to their rocks, she thought.

The majority of the locals didn't think much of the team of foreigners. The concept of someone making a living by studying rock formations was absurd to the agrarian mountain communities.

Yet that's exactly what they were doing. Geologists from four different nations, evaluating layers of asbestos deposits in the old Amiantos quarry. They had been working there for several weeks, and on that Wednesday morning in September they were returning to "their rocks" after having been confined to their cabins for way too long.

The sun was back in its rightful place on the blue horizon. Purple winter flowers were opening up and turning toward the source of the morning light. Birds interjected with their song. A stray brown dog sniffed the wet ground by Stalo's car on the side of the road.

After three days of heavy rains, the village was coming back to life again. Nature and people seemed to be returning to business as usual.

But it was not to last. Not for the geologists heading toward the quarry. Not for Stalo, engrossed in her household chores. Not for the 550 inhabitants of the village of Amiantos. Not for the nearby towns and cities. For all of Cyprus, it would not be business as usual. In fact, life on the island would never be the same again.

*   *   *

Mr. Davin Valois, Mr. Davin Valois, flight OS 831 to Larnaca, please proceed to gate G32. Your flight is boarding.

Monir Young ascended from the escalator near the business lounge to the departure level of the airport. He walked past the duty-free shops and the small specialty stores along the way. He moved briskly and purposefully, casting only a few sideways glances toward the travelers and products featured prominently in the storefronts. He made a brief stop at a café to purchase a pack of the famous Austrian Manner wafers—a favorite indulgence—and continued to his gate.

Monir believed that flying could be enjoyable for just a few categories of people: children, honeymooners, and vacationers. For those who filled airliners on a daily basis, flying was neither fun nor exciting. It was simply necessary, part of the job. And as the ace negotiator for CORE, a Swiss-based multinational with interests around the world, Monir's job required him to travel often. Flying business or first class certainly made things easier, but it was still work. Monir had already blocked out the movement of passengers and airport personnel around him. He munched on a wafer, his mind focused on his itinerary and the things he had to tend to upon his return to Geneva. He had been sitting near the gate counter when the speakers came on again, the alluring female voice capturing the attention of his business-traveler mind for just a moment.

Mr. Davin Valois, Mr. Davin Valois, flight OS 831 to Larnaca, please proceed to gate G32 immediately.

Without another thought to Mr. Valois's flight summons, Monir looked down at his watch. They should be starting to board his flight to Geneva any minute.

*　　*　　*

September: Cyprus

Rain was never convenient, but the villagers didn't complain. No one wanted repeats of droughts, water shortages, desalination plants, and imported drinking water being ferried by ships from Greece—conditions from the island's recent history. Rain was welcome in Cyprus. Always.

Even the geologists saw it positively. They'd been going hard for days, chiseling away at asbestos cliffs, obtaining samples, returning to their bungalow headquarters for testing, and writing detailed reports about their findings. The rain forced them to take a break, as they notified their supervisors back in England. But they made the most of their days of rest.

The team had largely remained in the cabins, playing cards and watching movies. Every few hours, two or three of them would jump into one of the rentals and head to Andrikkis, the village's grocery store, for snacks, drinks, and cigarettes.

Now, the rain finally having ended, they could resume work. Davin Valois had just taken the last sharp turn out of the village and begun the steady ascent to the Farmakas intersection, where they would head left toward the quarry. A young German researcher, Schom Friedrich, was riding shotgun.

"Nice-looking woman back there."

"Stalo. Stalo Leontiou. Pretty, eh? And nice...but Cypriot. She'd never go for a foreigner. Especially not you, Schom," Davin laughed, patting the German on the shoulder.

"You sure have a way of building people up, Davin," Schom joked.

The banter went on for a few more kilometers. The two women in the back—a Cambridge adjunct history professor and a Dutch Ph.D. student—remained quiet, rolling their eyes at their colleagues. Boys will be boys.

*   *   *

January: Vienna

For Monir, the most challenging part of travel had always been the waiting. For a ride to the airport. For luggage to be tagged. For security's approval at the X-ray scanners. For the long hours to pass before and between flights. For boarding to start. For the plane to fill up. For the flight to take off and land. For a ride to the hotel. For meetings in boardrooms to begin. For meals at restaurants to be prepared. Waiting was as inseparable a part of traveling as buying a ticket and packing a bag. It was always a factor. It was never enjoyable.

Generally, experienced travelers prepare for the wait so they can confront it productively. They tap away at their laptops or tablets. They read books or catch up on calls. Monir had established his own regimen for each wait-laden leg of the journey. While in lines at various checkpoints, he read emails and sorted them into appropriate folders—he had always insisted on maintaining a clean inbox. In airline lounges he nursed food and coffee and worked on his laptop. Magazine articles were reserved for the wait between boarding and takeoff. Books and additional computer work filled up the remainder of flight times, with short naps in between.

With his small carry-on and the latest issue of *Harvard Business Review* in hand—courtesy of the airport's business lounge—Monir scanned his boarding pass and joined the small group of fellow priority boarders. At the aircraft's entrance he greeted the flight attendants in German and walked to his seat in the business class section, stowing his bag in the overhead compartment.

Boarding continued at a steady rate. Other than a look and courteous nod at the woman who settled into the seat next to him, Monir was completely absorbed in his reading. The "boarding complete" announcement came through the intercom, and a smiling flight attendant began to offer refreshments to the passengers. Deciding what he wanted to drink, Monir folded his magazine and leaned forward to put it in the seat pocket in front of him.

At that exact moment, the female passenger in front of him leaned toward her seatmate and held her phone up for the man to see the text she had been writing. The motion catching his attention, Monir's eyes flicked up, glancing between the two headrests and landing on the phone.

He read the text. On any other day, Monir would not have paid it any attention. But on that day it registered clearly.

Davin Valois is done. Parkaus 3.

*   *   *

September: Cyprus

They entered the quarry around 8:45 AM. Despite the rains, the roads were generally passable, due to the packed gravel and stone. A few puddles, some rather deep, slowed down the convoy as drivers negotiated the terrain.

They ascended a winding road to the center of the quarry and turned right toward a slope adorned with young pines— part of the government's conservation program for the mountain that had been blasted and bulldozed down to a gray topographical eyesore.

The road continued along the front of an imposing asbestos rock face for two kilometers before curving around the northeastern edge of the quarry. According to their maps, just ahead would be the tallest peak of Amiantos, the location for that day's work.

After a hundred meters, the driver of the front SUV slammed on the brakes. All three cars came to a halt, skidding briefly on mud and gravel.

Just ahead of them the road ended abruptly where a huge chunk of mountainside had broken off. Dirt, boulders of asbestos, and small brush had fallen down the mountain into a ragged ravine. A wide, impassable chasm had formed between the geologists and the rest of the road.

The team exited the cars and walked to the edge of the newly formed cliff. They scanned their surroundings, bewildered. Exclamations ensued in their various languages.

Davin had been driving the front car, so he saw it first. Not just the washout, or the cliff, or the chasm. The stuff in the mountain. The non-asbestos material that was glistening beneath multiple layers of asbestos deposits.

Oblivious to the others still emerging from the SUVs, his eyes remained glued to the newly revealed cross-section of the mountain to his left. He walked slowly around the cliff, his mouth opening without speaking. His body language did the talking for him.

Before them lay a tightly packed vein of mineral deposits. The average person in the nearby villages, even those who had worked in the quarry before, may not have recognized the quartz-like material. But for Davin and at least a few members of his team, its identity was as clear as the Cyprus skies above them.

The material shining in the morning sun was not asbestos or the sedentary mica that was often found in shallow layers after the asbestos was quarried. The mineral was white from a distance, translucent up close. And after tests in their makeshift lab back at the bungalow, Davin's initial hunch was proven correct. It was lithium—what a number of publications had referred to as "the supermineral of the twenty-first century." And there was no telling how much of it they'd found.

* * *

January: Vienna

On the fourth floor of Parkaus 3, Vienna's long-term car park, a man's body lay still in a silver Mercedes. Blood flowed out of his left temple, sliding down his neck and onto the collar of his sport coat. He slumped across the center console. A few dozen cars were parked nearby, all of them empty.

The body was discovered by a couple returning to their car. The authorities arrived quickly and worked with characteristic Austrian efficiency. Several policemen dusted for fingerprints while a plainclothes officer took pictures from every angle.

The officer in charge opened the passenger door and squatted down until his eyes were almost parallel with the victim's upper body. He reached into the man's jacket and pulled out a French passport. He read the name aloud. "Davin Valois."

2

GAME-CHANGER

September: Amiantos, Cyprus

The geologists piled into the cars and left the site in a hurry. Davin spent most of the trip back to the village giving instructions. Once they arrived, Doug and Gloria would conduct the necessary tests; Anica, Thomas, and Francine would prep the samples; the rest of the team would get ready for further digs on the mountain and start the paperwork; Davin would make some calls.

Back at the cabin, Davin shouted one last admonition to his team: "And make sure absolutely no one hears about this!"

But before Davin and his team had even parked their vehicles back at their cabins, word about their find had started to spread. As the dust settled from the last RAV4 exiting the quarry, a man who was perched in a cabin several hundred feet north of the quarry's apex exchanged a mounted telescope for his handheld Canon, fitted with a 16-35mm f/2.8L II USM lens.

The man and a handful of other operatives, referred to as "Watchers" by their employer, had been keeping tabs on the geologists from the moment they had set foot on the island. He had already taken dozens of pictures of Davin and his team. Several clicks followed as he finished taking shots of the white mineral deposits left exposed to the mid-morning sun.

He picked up his iPhone, swiped, and tapped twice. In a few seconds he began to speak in German.

"This is Dietrich. They found it." He listened for a moment, his head bowed and tilted slightly, eyes fixed on the quarry below.

A question was posed on the other end.

"Yes, just like we thought," replied Dietrich.

Another question.

"They're gone. Took samples."

A short pause as information was conveyed to someone else in the room. "We expect them to move quickly, Dietrich. Keep your eyes open."

"Will do. Is that all?"

"Yes…but get Nadia in play as well. She knows what to do."

*   *   *

October: Troodos Mountain Range, Cyprus

A few weeks after their lithium find, Davin and his team of researchers began to venture northward, toward Troodos Mountain. Davin's superiors at the University of Cambridge had negotiated on his behalf and obtained a new set of clearances from the Cypriot government. The Ministry of Agriculture and Natural Resources had granted the team a license to dig at various locations on the Troodos Range. The stipulation was that non-disclosure agreements be signed, to keep any further findings under wraps. An official from the Mining Department would also have to be present at all the sites as a liaison between the geological team and the Ministry.

A GEOBOR S core drill was rented and shipped to Cyprus. The drill enabled Davin's team to obtain samples of mineral deposits from as deep as 200 meters below the earth's surface.

Within two weeks, the geologists had performed digs in many areas, including the outskirts of the Paphos Forest, the westernmost part of the 113-kilometer-long Troodos Range. As Davin had hoped, substantial lithium deposits were unearthed in every site. He kept his department head at Cambridge, Dr. Reginald Wiley, informed through daily email updates and frequent Skype sessions.

On a Thursday afternoon late in October, Davin could hardly contain his enthusiasm.

"Regi, I can't believe it! Lithium has turned up in GEOBOR's tubes from as deep as 150 meters almost everywhere we've drilled along the western slopes."

Dr. Wiley's mouth moved first in the slightly fuzzy image on Davin's screen. His voice followed momentarily. "That's incredible, Davin."

"Being that these are some of the lowest slopes on the Troodos Range, I can't even imagine the square footage of lithium that's packed in the higher elevations!"

"Astounding, indeed!"

Davin explained how the mineral was most compacted southwest of Mt. Olympus, Troodos's summit, along a ridge connecting the villages of Prodromos and Lemithou.

"Just from those digs alone, it's obvious that there's enough lithium embedded in these mountains to shift the world's hegemony of lithium supply away from China. And that's just the Troodos Range. Who knows what the Turks might have up north in the Pentadaktylos Mountain Range?"

"Well, let's not get ahead of ourselves here, Davin. One range at a time. We have our hands full with just Troodos."

After taking a few more notes, Dr. Wiley ended the conversation abruptly.

"Cheers, Davin. I need to speak with the Cypriot Minister of the Interior right away. Talk soon."

Dr. Wiley's talk with the Minister led to a barrage of phone conversations and private meetings over the next few days. Cabinet members, parliamentary leaders, business tycoons, bankers, and ultimately the Cypriot executive branch—including the president—were involved.

"For good reason!" Davin said when his colleague informed him of the development. "I've been doing my homework, Regi," he shouted into his cell phone over the noise of driving up the mountain early one Tuesday morning. "Lithium power plays a key role in automotive, aviation, and aerospace manufacturing. And lithium batteries are already used in lots of electronic devices that require a portable power supply."

"Right, Davin," Wiley said. "Companies are constantly trying to increase lithium batteries' output."

"Yes, and it isn't just batteries for devices," Davin continued. "Tesla's electric cars run on advanced lithium-ion batteries. Plus, up until now, homes and businesses haven't been able to store much of the power their solar cells generate. Lithium storage units will let people hold on to as much power as they want, either until they want to use it or until market prices are optimal to export or sell. Do you realize how important a major new supply of lithium will be for all this?"

"Sounds amazing, Davin."

Davin paused his monologue to take a breath and ensure Wiley was still on the line.

"I'm here, Davin."

"The market for this mineral is not just huge; it's massive. And the profit margins are significant enough to change the balance of power in world regions. Cyprus is perfectly positioned between Europe, the Middle East, and Eurasia to capitalize on one of the most potentially lucrative trades in history."

"I know this is big, Davin. More reason to make sure the team members keep quiet about it all. I'll keep monitoring the Cypriots as best I can."

Davin's repeated admonitions for secrecy, however, were proving useless. With the exception of any information exchanged while talking across the table in their bungalows, every bit of the team's progress was more widely known almost immediately. And neither Davin nor his Cambridge boss nor the Cyprus government had any idea about the breach.

The work on the Troodos Range continued. So did the back-and-forth with Cambridge. Davin and his team stayed on task, drilling, testing, logging, reporting. But something had been troubling Davin from the very beginning. He had decided to keep the matter to himself until he could look into it more closely.

In Davin's mind, rainfall, no matter how heavy, could not have brought down the sizeable asbestos-filled slope to expose the lithium below. The man had been a geologist at heart long before he pursued and obtained his degrees in geoscience at the Paris campus of the *Université Pierre et Marie Curie*. From the age of eight, Davin had given himself to exploring everything he could dig up under the grass in his backyard in the southern French town of Chapeiry.

During his adolescent years, while other kids went off to camps at the beautiful lakes and snowcapped mountains in the region, Davin spent his summers exploring rock formations with a retired geologist, a longtime friend of his father's. In his early twenties, Davin completed college, double majoring, then continued on to a master's and a Ph.D.

He filled in as an adjunct professor at a couple of European universities before securing his employment and, eventually, almost 15 years of tenure at Cambridge. At 45,

Davin Valois's understanding of mineral deposits and the rock formations surrounding them was unsurpassed.

Davin was well aware that the two largest mountain ranges in Cyprus, Troodos and Pentadaktylos, were once buried thousands of feet below the seabed, only emerging to the surface after eons of volcanic activity. Each violent eruption beneath the waves pushed up the growing, thickly packed layers of volcanic, sedimentary, and igneous rock. The landmass that constituted much of present-day Cyprus had reached the ocean's surface five million years ago. According to Davin's knowledge of Cyprus's turbulent geological history, all of Troodos was solid rock. No peak in its vicinity could have simply washed off due to rain.

Davin had remained private about his suspicions, mostly because he hadn't had time to investigate them. But a few days after confirming the substantial lithium deposits in the Troodos Range, the French scholar found the opportunity he needed. He broke away from the rest of the team early one Saturday morning and drove one of the SUVs back to the quarry. Armed with a shovel and his camera, Davin climbed down into the bottom of the ravine where the former asbestos mountainside had settled.

Within less than an hour of poking and minor digging, Davin's concerns were validated. Small pieces of charred wire were strewn in the area. Some were red, others pink.

One red wire was still connected to a damaged green plastic object resembling a plastic pen cap. Some of the dirt was strewn with ashes. A few bush roots that were sticking up out of the ground had burned tips. And several large boulders bore evidence of contact with gunpowder.

Peeking from beneath a sizeable rock was a yellow wire. Once Davin pushed away the rock, he found the remaining six inches of wire. It was almost intact and connected to another pen cap, this one blue. At the point where the wire fit into the plastic casing, he found a narrow tag bearing a bar code. He took pictures of everything, then coiled up the yellow wire and placed it in his pocket.

That afternoon, Davin put together a folder of all the pictures he had snapped up at the quarry. He attached the folder to an email he sent to Cambridge.

Regi, something to do with the site where we first found the mineral hasn't been right from the beginning. Found potentially substantial evidence to that effect today. Take a look. Let's talk ASAP.

Doug Thomson was Davin's most trusted colleague of the 10 geologists who had accompanied him to Cyprus. He had met the American during a conference at Yale back in the late '90s. Doug, a former environmental policy expert with the Army Rangers who was now a lecturer at Yale, had given a talk on the geological effects of cyclonic activity in the Pacific Rim. Davin was impressed by him right away. He asked if they could have lunch, and 15 years later they remained close friends.

The two academics had hosted each other numerous times for various conferences and forums at their respective universities. They had flown in together and had shared rooms both in Oslo and Brussels, where they attended councils as delegates. Doug and his wife, Bella, had even hosted Davin in their home several times.

Hours after he left the quarry, Davin was sitting across from Doug in his car, yellow wire in hand.

"I'm talking about an explosion, Doug. No idea who could be behind this or why, but during those days of heavy rain back in September, that asbestos slope was blown right off the rest of the mountain."

"How can you be so sure?" Doug's tone reflected worry rather than skepticism. He knew what Davin's allegations meant if they were accurate.

Davin walked Doug through the geological impossibility of the mountain slope suddenly eroding away. Doug nodded through all of it. Next, Davin showed Doug several pictures of the dirt, rocks, and charred colored wires.

"These remind me of the gummy-worm dirt cakes Bella used to make for the girls' birthdays," said Doug with a chuckle.

Davin broke into a grin, but he quickly turned his gaze to the yellow wire in his palm. He lifted his open hand slowly toward his friend. "What device does this belong to? You're the ex-military man."

Doug looked at the wire more closely.

"Explosives were not my specialty back in my army days, but I have a friend who knows a lot more. Maybe we should ask him."

"Who is it? Can we trust him?"

"Jeff Collins. We served in the Gulf together. He works out of Washington, D.C., for some government agency that deals with...forestry, I think. Great guy. Definitely trustworthy."

"OK. Hold on to the wire. I'm sure he'll want to see it."

*   *   *

Washington, D.C., USA

As planned, Doug placed a call to Jeff Collins. After a few minutes of catching up, Doug got to the point. He informed his friend of the lithium find and of the wires Davin found.

"We think it may be part of some sort of explosive device. Let me try to describe it for you."

Jeff's face had turned serious the moment Doug described the pen cap. Keeping his voice calm, he asked for some pictures of the wire. Doug forwarded the pictures; when they arrived a few minutes later, Jeff's hunch was confirmed.

Even so, he remained coy. "Give me some time to figure this out, Doug. I'll try to run the barcode too."

The barcode was just a formality at that point. Jeff knew exactly what they were dealing with, and his expertise gave him the advantage of time—a rare luxury in his line of work.

The yellow wire belonged to a blasting system produced by a company in Finland. The plastic pen caps housed time-delay, in-hole detonators, which were in turn wrapped with explosives such as C4 or TNT. Used primarily in mining and quarrying, the charges were lowered into drilled holes or natural crevices, depending on the magnitude of the desired blast. Jeff's Ranger battalion had used the system in Kuwait, during the First Gulf War, to shake up enemy installations with underground explosions.

Jeff had completed his research a few hours after talking to Doug. Then he picked up the phone and placed two calls. One was local; the other was to Tel Aviv.

As Davin continued to send email updates to his superiors at Cambridge, all lithium-related progress on the mountains of Cyprus was tracked, processed, and recorded on a laptop in Vienna. A team of two Watchers had been observing Davin closely for months.

Earlier that year, Viktor and Kristal, both Austrian residents, had flown to England. Posing as Cambridge students, they had hacked into Davin's laptop from the back of a lecture hall. While Professor Valois was presenting facts about earthquakes in his Earth Sciences course, the hackers began to receive an exclusive feed into Davin's personal and professional life.

For the next few weeks, they monitored his emails closely, logging every detail on a master flowchart in their Vienna apartment. Kristal intercepted the departmental approval for Davin's asbestos research on the island of Cyprus, as well as his emails to the 10 team members who would accompany him. Viktor was the first to see the approval of Davin's application for geological studies at Amiantos. Orestis Sophroniou, the director of Cyprus's Mining Department of the Ministry of Agriculture and Natural Resources, had even ended his letter with a friendly *Kopiaste*—Greek for "welcome." Little did the authorities know that Davin's welcome letter was a long-awaited cue for his Watchers to mobilize for the next phase of their objective.

Following Davin's email to Dr. Wiley after finding the wires at the quarry, the Vienna Watchers eagerly waited for a follow-up email. It came about a week later. As promised, Jeff Collins had called Davin to give him his verdict on the wires. Then Davin sent an email to Wiley, explaining the matter.

My contact confirmed it, Regi. The colored wires are remnants of explosives. Someone blew up the mountain, possibly to expose the lithium.

*   *   *

Farrouk Ahmadi was in Brussels, having coffee with a European-looking woman, when his phone buzzed. He looked down at Davin's email, forwarded to him from Vienna. Without a word of explanation or apology to the woman—she seemed bored rather than bothered—he read the email's contents and replied: an email to Vienna, then a scolding text to his Watchers in Cyprus.

*   *   *

Upon receiving Farrouk's text, Dietrich was nervous and agitated. "Farrouk says it's time. She needs to make her move, right now!"

"Take it easy," his partner, Yury, shot back. "We had to know where he stood on everything first. Now that the Frenchman has shown his colors, we make our move. Simple."

"The Frenchman knows. How much does he know? Who has he spoken to? We have to find out! Then we clean up. Make the call—now!"

*　　*　　*

Koilani, Cyprus

Nadia knew exactly where to find Davin.

Viktor and Kristal had also dissected details about Davin's world beyond academia. Experience had taught them that information about a target's personal life would come in handy sooner or later. Davin was a wine connoisseur, they'd discovered, and his passion for the fruit of the vine offered the best opportunity for Nadia's entrance. Viktor had pored over several emails in which Davin raved to family and friends about the various Cypriot wineries he had visited during his first few weeks on the island.

On the Friday after the lithium discovery, Davin had written a Cambridge colleague about his exciting weekend coming up, complete with a visit to Vlasides Winery at Koilani village. *This ought to be fantastic,* Davin wrote. *Vlasides's Shiraz is by far the best in Cyprus, perhaps the entire Med!*

On Saturday morning, Dietrich followed Davin and the two other geologists who had chosen to accompany him. Davin drove their RAV4 southwest towards Moniatis. At the Saittas intersection, Dietrich's Nissan rental turned right, toward Troodos, while Yury entered the scene with a blue Toyota truck. From about 100 meters back, he followed Davin the rest of the way through Pera Pedi and Agia Mavri to Koilani. When the SUV took a left into Vlasides's winery, the Watcher continued straight. He called Nadia.

Nadia began to drive her red Range Rover Evoque from her stakeout at Vouni, a few kilometers south of the winery. She moved toward Koilani at a steady speed, and within minutes she pulled into a parking spot across from Davin's at the winery.

Inside, a Vlasides employee was wrapping up the tour. Davin and his colleagues were just about to start the wine tasting. Nadia walked up the concrete steps to the front entrance, opened the glass door, and entered the room where everyone had gathered.

She was wearing light gray skinny jeans and black boots. A black leather jacket covered most of the bright yellow blouse that offered cleavage views to wandering eyes. Her dark brown hair was pulled back, a few strands loose in the front accenting her green eyes.

She nodded at the tour guide and Davin's group. With a big smile and an unmistakable Russian accent, she said, "I hope I haven't missed the Shiraz. It's just the best!"

3
ASSIGNMENTS

January: Geneva

Monir disembarked behind the couple who'd been sitting in front of him. Acting disinterested, he stole a few glances at them as they walked off the aircraft.

The man was tall and thin with black hair. He wore a tan leather jacket over charcoal designer jeans. His partner had straight bleached hair with jet-black roots—a style for which a salon must have charged quite a premium. Purple silk encircled her neck and settled neatly around the collar of her red suede jacket. Her silver-blue high-heeled boots made a statement of their own.

As the passengers headed for the gate, the woman turned to the man. About to speak, she instinctively shot a sideways look at the passenger closest to them, ensuring he couldn't overhear. It was Monir. Indeed, he couldn't hear a thing. He only saw her lips move for a second and her head turn forward again.

Her companion reached into his pocket and pulled out his phone, tapping on the screen.

By now the distance between Monir and the couple had widened. He took out his own phone and held it in front of him, tapping on the screen briefly. Unlike the man, Monir wasn't texting. He was snapping pictures. His instincts told him there was something suspicious about these two; his experience told him that remembering what they looked like might prove useful.

Between the escalator—where Nespresso was soliciting coffee drinkers through a massive poster of a smiling George Clooney—and the Swiss watch ads lining the walls on both sides, Monir shot six pictures of the couple. He also managed two front shots while waiting for luggage directly across from them at Carousel 4.

At the curb, he swiped through the photos, deleting three pictures he deemed redundant. Minutes later, in his cab, Monir created a folder called "Davin Valois" and moved the remaining pictures into it. Then he texted his boss to notify him of his arrival.

Mid-morning Geneva weather was ideal. Seasonably cold, yet beautiful. Bright skies and low humidity. Mont Blanc, though more than 80 kilometers away, seemed to be right on the other side of the lake.

Just like the photo file he had created earlier, Monir mentally filed away the events surrounding his flight from Vienna. He looked straight ahead at the city, his mind consumed with thoughts of opening mail, dinner, much-needed rest, and the pile of work undoubtedly waiting for him at the office.

The rest of the winter passed uneventfully for Monir. With the exception of following up on a few leads for emerging gemstone markets in the South Pacific and his annual trip to Brussels for the International Quarry and Mine Convention, he kept himself busy by filing paperwork and maintaining key relationships over phone or Skype.

Generally, Monir was the happiest at CORE when he was representing the company overseas. As challenging as travel could be, he loved to see new places and experience what different cultures had to offer. But the greatest reason Monir thrived while being away was he didn't have to deal with the company's CEO, Karl Braun.

For as long as the two men had worked together, Monir had been uncomfortable around his boss, feeling as though Braun always had a hidden agenda. The CEO would inform Monir of a project at hand and the part he was expected to have in it, but Braun would leave out details he often referred to as "stage-preparation procedures." Monir had done enough digging of his own over the years to learn that CORE routinely placed numerous people on the same project but deliberately prevented those individuals from operating as a team. Most of the time, the people didn't even know each other. Everyone recognized there were other parts contributing to the whole, but they were told only to be concerned with their specific tasks, to never look into matters that other operators were handling. Monir tried to address the matter with Braun, stating that such practices could foster disunity and mistrust, but the boss always brushed Monir's concerns aside with vague remarks like "The stellar performance of the company over time proves that the ends do indeed justify the means."

Monir also felt tense when weeks would go by without any communication from Braun beyond greetings and niceties around the office. Not that Monir had need of quality time with his employer, but, historically, the longer the period before their last assignment-related conversation, the worse the next interaction would be. During the four months since his return from Vienna—a season when he and Braun had spoken minimally—Monir felt sure that a challenging encounter was looming on the horizon.

Sure enough, on an afternoon in late May, the CEO asked to see Monir in his office, with little warning. As meticulous as the German CEO was about most things, he never scheduled his meetings with field agents. If they were in the building, Braun buzzed them and asked to meet within a half hour or so. Among other things, that particular habit had always bothered Monir; however, there was nothing he could do about it.

"Cyprus?" Monir said. "Really, Karl, have you been following the news the last few years? Nice beaches and all, but from a business standpoint, the place is a dump. Government corruption, money laundering, bankruptcy, banks closing—do I need to continue?"

Monir had an amazing ability to dial down as the conversation intensified. He had developed the skill over many years of discussing sensitive matters behind closed doors. By the time he posed his last question to Braun, Monir was almost whispering.

Karl, knowing Monir well, answered with a near-whisper of his own. "Yes, keep going. All these things are true, but keep going until you see what lies beneath the country's geopolitical rubble. Opportunity, Monir, extraordinary opportunity!"

Monir knew exactly what that meant. To Braun and all of CORE's top brass, he was the man who could find and seize opportunity in even the worst of circumstances. His most notable deal, and the source of his legendary status in the company, had been securing gold-mining contracts in Ghana. In 2006, he and Carmela, a female CORE associate, had flown down to the Volta region after CORE received a tip about gold in land that spanned the two districts of Akatsi and Ketu.

Through lavish gifts and strategic bribes, Monir quickly found his way to the tribal leaders who, in spite of the general oversight of the Regional Coordinating Council and the administration of the district assembly, still called the shots in most of rural Ghana.

Monir's handouts were complimented by Carmela's flirting. The ambitious 27-year-old brunette from Milan quickly let it be known that she was not attached to Monir romantically and was therefore quite available. Over drinks and dances, she managed to acquire all necessary information about the influence and corruptibility of the decision makers. Carma, as she was known at CORE, had a remarkable ability to seduce without committing. During the six weeks she worked Ghana with Monir, she was seen with a dozen different men, yet she did not sleep with any of them.

With Carma's help and more than eight million Ghanaian cedi in bribes to tribal leaders, Monir secured a mining contract with local and regional authorities, even with the endorsement of the Precious Minerals Marketing Corporation, the government entity responsible for promoting and marketing gold and diamond mining in the nation. They agreed that CORE would employ and fairly compensate miners from five nearby villages. Moreover, it would build three schools and drill several water wells in the region. That was, of course, the legitimate part of what would become a multibillion-dollar deal.

Several similar scenarios—though none quite as profitable—unfolded in different corners of the globe: gold and copper in Egypt; silver in Chile; gemstones and gold in East Timor; ruby and sapphire mines in Myanmar.

Karl adjusted his Gold and Wood rimless glasses. "This is big, Monir," he said. "We don't have any room for learning curves here. You're the man who knows best how to get this done. I have an advance team there already. Everything is almost in place. You're going to Cyprus to close this deal, and this will be our greatest hour yet!"

As the words left his lips, Karl raised his hands and gestured out his office window. He hoped Monir's eyes would follow his to the vastness of the view before them. From the sixth floor of CORE's state-of-the-art offices near the corner of Rue du Rhone and Passage de la Monnaie, Lake Geneva shimmered at the base of the majestic Alpine backdrop, offering the perfect scenery for bold statements and hopeful declarations.

Monir's gaze remained on the bookcase next to Karl's desk. He was going on 23 years with CORE and was familiar with Karl's persuasion tactics. He was also aware that Karl had just given him an order.

Karl Braun had been the CEO of CORE for as long as Monir had been on the job. With special focus in the area of foreign mining assets, Braun had orchestrated CORE's steady ascent to prominence. But though he ran the company, Braun masterfully convinced his subordinates that it was their contributions that counted most. "A leader can only be as successful as the outstanding people who surround him," he would say during annual CORE employee conferences. But Karl's capable, charismatic leadership, as well as his longstanding record of progress, was helped by the fact that he owned more stock in the company than any other single individual. Karl Braun did not work for CORE; for all intents and purposes, he *was* CORE.

Monir finally looked at his boss. Karl was still feigning a contemplative gaze at the lake and mountains beyond. "I go alone," Monir said. "I work alone." When Karl turned around, Monir spoke briefly but with confidence. "I'm much more comfortable negotiating without the presence of sideshows."

Karl smiled, letting Monir know that his request had just been granted. Monir could do Cyprus alone. Results were CORE's primary language, and Monir spoke it fluently.

The funds for CORE's gifts-and-bribes program came from one of its secret slush funds. Surprisingly, the Geneva-based company did not utilize a Swiss bank but a Cypriot one: Cyprus Sovereign Bank. The account was nicknamed the "Thumb Fund" because the branch Monir's bosses used was located at a busy intersection the locals called Pentadromos, or "five roads."

Giannis Theodorou, the branch manager, had been the one to alert Karl about the lithium find. The two corporate leaders had been engaged in a mutually beneficial and fully illegal operation for years. They met in the early '90s, when Karl went on a mini-European tour, fishing for a new bank in which to stash money that would finance handouts. A friend of his brother's had mentioned Cyprus Sovereign Bank, an institution friendly to foreign companies looking to avoid prying eyes.

"Accounts can be opened without questions regarding the purpose for the account or the origin of the funds," the friend told Karl in between swigs of Pielsner at a Budapest bar. "And the manager is a very discrete man. A climber. He knows and plays the game rather well."

Within months, Karl had made four trips to the bank, each time with several briefcases full of euros and U.S. dollars. Over the next decade or so, Theodorou and his bank branch had facilitated the laundering of millions of euros and dollars, most of which was used for greasing wheels in corrupt governments and for acquiring lucrative deals. For his services—he often personally handled Karl's transactions from his office—Theodorou had received over 300,000 Swiss francs, 50,000 shares of CORE stock, a rare rose gold Rolex Cellini, and a five-star vacation to Majorca with his wife.

Come to Cyprus, quickly, he wrote Karl through an encrypted email on an unseasonably cold Tuesday in October, just weeks after Davin and his team had discovered the lithium. *Major opportunity here. Someone you need to meet.*

Monir was vaguely aware of Braun's Cyprus banking connection, yet until that point he had been unfamiliar with the particulars of Braun's October meeting with Theodorou.

As Karl now explained to Monir, he had always executed most of the financial details of CORE's operations from Cyprus, but he had never conducted any business *in* Cyprus.

Until October 29th, that is, when Theodorou had made the introduction to a government employee he referred to as "one of my best friends."

"We had lunch at Hobo Meditteraneo by the newly built Limassol Marina—you should go there, Monir," Karl said. "The new acquaintance was Angelos Mavros, and he lost no time in getting to the point." Karl paused for a bit as he paced along his bookcase. Then he continued to recount the meeting with Mavros.

There was lithium to be had—lots of it. The deal would go to the highest bidder, and very soon. Mavros spoke for about three minutes. He used excellent English and spoke softly and calmly. He used short sentences, looking Karl straight in the eye the entire time.

"And that is the amazing thing about some of these corrupt Cypriots," Karl noted. "They all started out by being honest, hard-working, sincere employees of a government they believed in. Somewhere along the way, be it due to unsatisfied ambition or greed, they embraced the dark side of the system. But amazingly, they have managed to maintain some of the qualities they had throughout their honest careers—in this case the unblinking, trust-earning eyes. Strange, but it works for us."

"What did you say to this man?"

"I asked him whether the lithium find was verified," Karl said, "and whether a mining contract could be made available to our company through an agreement between us."

"The deal will go to the highest bidder," Mavros had reiterated, slowly tapping a business card against the table. "The entire Troodos Mountain—perhaps the Troodos Range altogether—is sitting on lithium. We believe the Americans, Russians, and of course our Turkish neighbors are all here to grab a deal."

Karl told Monir how impressed he was at Mavros's cool demeanor. "He had done this before, you can be sure of that."

Mavros continued with the details. "We can arrange for CORE to sit at a private negotiating table. 300,000 euros, cash, for the party hosts—business associates of ours who will arrange for a nice dinner at their summer home in Protaras."

"And for you?"

"Two million francs in the Zurich account on the back of this card." Mavros had laid his card on the table. Then, looking Braun straight in the eye, he slid the card over to him.

"Half up front, half after CORE signs the deal with our government."

"I looked at the card, then back up at Mavros," Braun told Monir. "I must say, I had a fleeting thought about potentially recruiting the Cypriot for other projects in the future."

Monir thought for a moment and then asked, "Did he say how much the mineral was worth?"

Karl smiled. He was pleased that Monir was engaging in the matter with questions. "When I asked, Mavros responded immediately, as though he'd been waiting for the question all day. He said he'd looked up the public records of CORE's earnings for the last 10 years."

"And?" Monir asked.

"The lithium deal will procure more than all of it combined."

Briefed about the scenario in Cyprus—mostly from the research Karl's team was supplying from the field—Monir tied up some loose ends in the office and prepared to head to Cyprus himself.

On May 29th, Monir checked two pieces of luggage at the Swiss Airlines First Class counter and made his way through security. He'd be at his rented condo, deep in the mountains of Cyprus, before the end of the day.

4

THE PLAYERS

November: Kyrenia (Girne), Cyprus

"What do you mean, 'bigger than the gas?'"

Mahmoud Giarlou looked at the mayor intensely. Mayor Evrim Aydim had called for the meeting when he heard the Turkish ambassador would be in town to speak at a conference.

"Just what I said. The potential of this deal is greater than that of the natural gas the Cypriots found in the sea bottom. Actually, the mineral is more promising than any other resource this island has ever had to offer."

He proceeded to fill in Ambassador Giarlou about the lithium find, laying out the scenario that had unfolded in Troodos.

Giarlou did not respond right away. He looked in the direction of the scenic port, then Kyrenia Castle. Not much had changed in that idyllic spot since the Turkish invasion of 1974 and the subsequent occupation of the island's northern regions.

Eyes on Evrim, Giarlou picked up his phone and placed the call. "This could change everything." It was ringing in the other end. "Everything!"

The mayor nodded and took a puff from his cigarette. "Who are you calling?"

Giarlou, almost at the end of his own cigarette, kept his eyes on the castle and filled the space between him and Aydim with smoke as he responded. "The president."

* * *

Larnaca Airport, Cyprus

"And what is the nature of your visit here in Cyprus, Mr. and Mrs…Av-dey-ev?" The immigration officer managed a smile to cover for her butchering of the names.

"Vacation," the man said with a thick Russian accent and a smile at his wife. The woman nodded and smiled as well. "Yes, vacation."

Two stamps in rapid succession and a longer smile from the officer. "Enjoy your stay."

Without any luggage except their carry-ons, Vasily and Darya Avdeyev walked briskly past the customs area and approached the arrivals hall in the lower level of Larnaca's airport. The driver holding an "Avdeyev" sign spotted them first. He was familiar with his clients as were they with him. In fact, he could have waited in the car, but appearances were important in front of airport cameras.

The couple stopped and scanned the signs that various drivers were holding up. Darya pretended to have spotted their man and pointed. Vasily played the part perfectly and nodded with an "O, da." The driver came around and greeted them.

"Welcome," he said in English with a Cypriot accent. "I take you." He picked up their small, matching Tumi carry-on spinners and headed for the escalator.

No one spoke again until they were in the car. The driver opened the doors, loaded the luggage in the rear, and settled into his seat. He immediately switched to flawless Russian.

"I hope your flight was pleasant. Dimitry is expecting you."

"Good," Darya responded.

Vasily was on his phone, and though it was completely safe to do otherwise, he spoke in low tones. "On the ground. No problems. Heading to Dimitry."

A case officer on the other end hung up the phone. He looked at the two men sitting in the leather armchairs as he placed his phone back on the desk. "They're in."

* * *

Langley, Virginia, USA

The sliding glass doors closed behind the director with a characteristic swoosh and a final clasp of exclusivity. He entered the conference room and moved briskly and purposefully toward his seat at the head of the long mahogany table.

"Keep your seats," he said, his eyes darting around the room for a quick assessment. Those who had started to stand sat back in their brown leather swivel chairs, all eyes on him. The rest seemed glad they had stayed put. Navy blue folders were lying in front of everyone, and they all knew better than to look inside before he started.

Still standing, the director placed his hand on the lower edge of his folder and looked at the group.

"Ladies and gentlemen, it has been confirmed by our Turkey, Greece, and Middle East station chiefs that much of Cyprus is sitting on top of lithium. One of our agents from Washington has information about a potential conspiracy. We're already in the process of mobilizing a team from Munich, and we are mobilizing other assets for any information they can obtain."

He opened his folder and paused long enough to scan the faces of the agents sitting closest to him. He looked back down and adjusted his glasses. "There's a lot to do, and we have to move quickly. Let's get to work."

*　　*　　*

Following Nadia's attention-grabbing entrance at the winery, she and Davin had spent a few hours sharing wine and swapping wine-related knowledge—and later swapping numbers. The Frenchman decided to call her the next day from Troodos during a break from drilling.

He took out his phone and found her number under the name she had given him: Myra Kortelli. Nadia's voicemail message kicked in immediately. "Hi, you've reached Myra. Please leave a message. Ciao."

Davin left a short message. He was careful to show the necessary interest without coming across as an infatuated college student, though that was exactly how he felt inside.

Myra called Davin within the hour. They talked for a long time. The next night they met for dinner in Limassol. Things moved quickly after that.

Over dinners by the ocean and late-night drinks at the balcony table of her high-rise apartment, Davin quickly became smitten by Myra. He loved everything about her: Russian-born but raised in Milan by her Italian father after her mother died in a car accident. Beautiful. Stylish. Creative.

As she told Davin on their first date together, she had finished a master's in sociology, yet had chosen to thrust herself into the world of fashion design. She said it wasn't long before she became prominent in her field, being sought after within the higher echelons of the European glamour industry. Myra claimed she wasn't flattered when a high-level staffer with Hugo Boss or Armani would call while she and Davin were dining together or driving to yet another scenic spot on the island. She'd often reach and take hold of Davin's hand throughout the call's duration. Phone pressed against her ear, she'd look at Davin and silently mouth the name of the designer on the other end. Then she'd roll her eyes and wink.

All of it was untrue—part of Nadia's flashy cover story designed to lure Davin in.

Beyond her beauty and intrigue, what also captivated Davin was how much he and Myra had in common, from Vlasides Shiraz to favorite foods, movies, books. They talked extensively of fantasy travel destinations, dream car makes (even colors!), ideological positions, and views about world matters. He was fast turning head over heels for her, as she was definitely a lover of the finer things…and, within just a few dates, a lover of his.

Late one Thursday night, after spending the afternoon with Davin at the Amathus Beach Hotel spa, Nadia—

shedding her identity as Myra Kortelli the moment she entered her apartment—sat on the spacious veranda that overlooked the Mediterranean waters near Limassol's port. Across from her sat Dietrich and Yury.

With one hand, Nadia was holding a glass of vodka; with the other, she was scrolling down an intercepted email that she was reading aloud. The team in Vienna had already translated the content into English. Nadia got to the part she particularly wanted the others to hear, looked up, and paused for effect. It was Davin's closing remark to his brother Pierre, back in France: *This one's a keeper. We're a perfect match for each other!*

Yury chuckled; the German grinned. They both took swigs from their beer bottles. Nadia looked out over the balcony that faced the black horizon, watching the few lit-up ships that would be docking portside the next morning. She took a sip of her drink. Just then, the waves crashed on the shore below. She heard the sound as applause. In her mind, if the email she had just finished reading constituted a progress report on her assignment, Davin's last line was a straight A.

The Turkish government responded to the news of the lithium find on Troodos in a predictable manner, as far as the Cypriot government was concerned. The president sent a delegation to Nicosia, Cyprus's capital, to reopen talks for a "quick and just" resolution to the 40-year diplomatic gridlock that had followed the 1974 invasion and subsequent division of the island. Any progress made over the years had resembled New York City traffic around Christmas; however, now was "the dawn of a new day—the start of a new era of cooperation between our countries," as the Turkish president said in a press release in Ankara.

Turkish negotiators pitched an unprecedented deal, offering the reopening of the Turkish-occupied cities of Kyrenia and Famagusta for Greek Cypriots. Former owners of homes and businesses would be able to return to their properties, to settle among the existing Turkish Cypriot population of those cities, as the Turkish government was prepared to honor pre-1974 title deeds. Moreover, Turkey promised "jurisdictional autonomy" for Cypriots returning to their lands, a most vague, and ultimately unattainable, model of governance whereby Greek Cypriots would abide by Cypriot law in the land Turkey had conquered and was referring to as the "Turkish Republic of Northern Cyprus."

In return, as one delegate from Ankara stated during a meeting in Famagusta, Turkey offered to work with the Cypriot government toward the best ways to maximize the economic and strategic potential of the mineral deal.

Centuries of mistrust and 40 years of dead ends in negotiations made the Cypriot government apprehensive about the offer. The Cypriot newspaper *Phileleftheros* responded to the Ankara press release with a front-page article in which the Turkish overtures were dismissed as "surface niceties targeting hidden treasures"—a comment that caused concern for Cypriot officials, as the lithium find was supposed to be under wraps. Cyprus's president told his foreign minister to keep the door open but stall. He hoped other major players would soon come forth with an offer that would give Cyprus more leverage with the Turks.

All the while, a Turkish quarry, operating on behalf of the government, ordered two GEOBOR drills from Austria, and within weeks Turkey began to drill in the 80-kilometer-long Pentadaktylos Mountain Range in search of lithium.

None was found.

*   *   *

Pedoulas, Cyprus

During their time together, Davin had told Myra about his geological digs up on the mountains, but he had remained very discreet regarding the lithium find. He spoke of his daily progress vaguely, using broad strokes such as "we're looking into some possibilities with one particular mineral" and "nothing is definite as of yet."

Davin was guarded partly due to the non-disclosures he'd signed and partly because he was afraid Myra would be uninterested. Myra, however, expressed great interest whenever Davin spoke of his work. She asked questions and pressed in for meaningful talk—but only to a point. Farrouk's instructions had been clear from the beginning: "Don't go too far, Nadia. Your part is to keep him talking about his work. His part, unbeknownst to him, is to trust you more every day until you're the closest one to him."

Over the five years she had served her employers at CORE, Nadia had played similar roles with several men. The stakes, the context, and the men's nations and cultures had all been different, but the game was always the same. Enter the target's life through manipulation and deceit, acquire a decent understanding of his psyche, and strategically leverage the man's strengths and weaknesses to serve her objectives. Nadia had learned that some variables were identical regardless of the person or context. For one, her chances of getting a man to talk were much greater when alcohol, sex, or trouble was involved.

Lovemaking with Davin had already gone as far as Nadia was willing to take it, and the Frenchman wasn't given to drunkenness, despite his love of wine. Nadia recommended that her bosses "push the trouble button" in Davin's life, and Farrouk and Karl Braun agreed.

Late in November, Dietrich and Yury took a 50-minute drive to the outskirts of the village of Pedoulas, where Davin's team had started drilling a few days earlier. Following the directions given to them by CORE's Vienna intelligence team, they found the GEOBOR early in the morning. Unloading a small bag from the trunk, they went to work.

The Watchers did not seriously harm the drill itself. The damage was only to get Davin's attention. Once he was on-site and without a working drill, he would surely look around enough to notice the colored wires the two saboteurs had strategically scattered near the drill hole.

The objective was to give Davin enough of a shock that he would open up to his lover about it. The Watchers aimed to find out what Davin may have learned about the wires, and more importantly, who else he may have spoken to.

As Dietrich had tried to explain to Yury while they were loading the car to head up the mountain, "If you don't remember how your dog reacted when you fed him a certain food, feed him the same food again and watch."

Though the analogy was gibberish to the Russian, he finished planting the wires and got back in the car. They were back in Limassol long before first light.

The plan could not have worked better. Davin was alerted about the damaged drill by a couple of colleagues who arrived on the site early that morning. He rushed to Pedoulas, where he saw the broken-down drill. He then spent much of the morning making phone calls to locate a repairman. The government employee who had been assigned to shadow the operation recommended his wife's second cousin. "He's a good mechanic. Works mostly on tractors and bulldozers, but he can fix this." The man was rushed up the mountain from Nicosia and was fast at work by noon.

Having lost the first part of the morning already, and having little hope that the drill would be repaired before the day's end, Davin began to change his afternoon and evening plans. First he called an aide from the Ministry of the Interior and asked if they could postpone their appointment to go over drilling protocols. Then he canceled his four-o'clock meeting with members of his team. They had planned to meet in Limassol to have coffee and discuss the plan for the digs after Pedoulas.

Lastly, he called Myra.

"I'm really sorry to do this to you...having a rotten morning. I probably won't be down till late."

"No problem, Davin. What's the matter? Is everything OK? You sound stressed." Nadia smiled at Dietrich, who smiled back and began to text an update to Farrouk.

"Our drill's been down since the start of the day, but they're working on it. I'll fill you in later, OK?"

"Of course. And please let me know if there's anything I can do."

"Thanks, Myra. Means a lot to me."

"*You* mean a lot to *me*."

That night, Davin sat across from the beautifully dressed and exceptionally empathetic Myra Kortelli. She had made a reservation at The Yacht Club, insisting the maître d' show them to a corner table that offered a spectacular view of the marina beyond.

She gave Davin space at first, waiting for him to broach the subject. Halfway through his second glass of Chablis, Davin began to open up. He told Myra he had decided to take her into his confidence and share some details about his work with her. While Myra picked at a salad, keeping her eyes mostly on him, Davin told her everything—the lithium find, the drilling process, the geopolitical implications, the boss back in England, and, of course, the troubles of that day. "Thankfully, the problem was minor," he said. "The drill should be ready to go in the morning."

Myra called a waitress over and ordered a bottle of red wine. *The night is still young,* she thought to herself.

Myra propped a pillow against the headboard and sat up in her bed, still breathing heavily from her exertion. Davin was next to her, doing the same. As with most of the nights they'd spent together, the date had ended at Myra's apartment. First, they'd had a nightcap together; then they'd engaged in passionate sex.

Davin was sitting with his back to Myra, looking at the night skies beyond her balcony doors. "There's something else."

"Something else? About what?"

"About today. Something else happened up there. I found something."

Lying down next to Myra, Davin began to speak, his eyes on the ceiling. He described the colored wires he'd found that morning near the GEOBOR, telling her how they were identical to some other wires he'd found up at Amiantos quarry shortly after they found the lithium there.

Myra put on a bathrobe and sat in a chair opposite the bed. She listened intently, occasionally taking a sip of her scotch. When Davin finished talking, Myra faced the sea beyond her open window, pretending to ponder what he had just shared. Then she asked the question she'd been working toward all night. "This sounds very suspicious. Have you talked to anyone about it?"

*   *   *

Nicosia, Cyprus

The three-meter-tall metal gate slowly slid open. A green Mitsubishi Pajero rolled past the American guard post, where a Marine stood at attention, saluting the driver. Then the diesel 4WD inched through the open gate and headed for the glass-encased guard post that was manned by an armed Cypriot officer. The side window slid open and the guard handed the Pajero's driver a clipboard. The man signed the document and returned it to the guard, who in turn bent forward for a quick glance at the driver and his passenger. He gave a half-baked two-finger salute before he slid the window shut.

At the embassy's street checkpoint, the driver waived at two uniformed guards and turned left onto Metochiou

Street. At the light, another left, onto Ploutarchou. Up ahead was the first sign for Strovolos/Troodos.

"Wanna stop for coffee?" the driver asked his female passenger.

She was running her fingers through her wet hair, wishing she'd gotten up earlier to get ready. The first morning overseas was always that way for her. "Nah, we can get some later. Unless you want it."

He looked down at the GPS as they passed the Russian embassy on their right.

"Says we'll be at Amiantos in 45 minutes. Plenty of time for coffee. Keep an eye out for a café."

He had arrived three days before she did. According to his passport, he was 36-year-old Andrew Remington from Mora, Minnesota. His embassy credentials identified him as a custodial services supervisor.

She had entered Cyprus, not even 24 hours earlier, as Rene Fletcher from Portland, Oregon. Her embassy file stated she was single, 39, and serving at the visa department of the consulate.

Actually, Tyson and Cynthia Blake were in their early 40s. They had met during training at the covert CIA training facility known as "The Farm," tucked away within the confines of Camp Peary, Virginia, and had married in 2005, shortly after being stationed at the Agency's field office in Munich.

They had received their orders two weeks prior, and they'd mobilized accordingly after receiving numerous briefings and their new aliases. Neither Tyson nor Cynthia would occupy themselves with custodial or consular work. Their assignment was of a completely different nature.

5

DITCH ENCOUNTER

May: Cyprus

Monir had been assured by Braun that the lithium deal was already settled. All he had to do was nurture a few key relationships and appear at a meeting between Cypriot government officials and a team of attorneys and representatives from the banking sector.

More than two decades in the field had taught Monir some valuable lessons. He had learned the hard way, particularly through a botched deal over diamond mines in South Africa, that the outcome of negotiations is never fully determined away from the negotiating table. The boss may have insisted the lithium contract was as good as signed, but Monir's experience prompted him to approach the matter with as much preparation and diligence as the toughest of deals.

Two hours after he arrived at Larnaca International Airport, Monir was standing in front of his two-bedroom rental in the mountain village of Agios Mamas. CORE's international logistics team had worked their magic once again. The condo was situated atop the highest peak of the village, with a stunning view of Troodos Mountain. A fruit basket sat on the kitchen table next to a bottle of 2002 Tsiakkas Sauvignon Blanc. A small white card was wedged between a nectarine and an apple: *Welcome, my friend. I hope everything is to your liking. Farrouk.*

Monir took no time to enjoy the wine or fruit. Neither did he explore the house or take in the scenery beyond his bedroom window. He unpacked, showered, and lied down for a quick nap, intending to be up before the afternoon was gone. He would drive out to Amiantos quarry and to some of the other sites where lithium had turned up in significant quantities, to check things out for himself. Another lesson the years had taught him: The more he learned from personal research, the greater his advantage at the negotiating table.

Heading for the quarry, it didn't take long for Monir to become hopelessly lost. He was struggling to keep an eye on the road while he tried to pull up a map on his phone. Then, with a loud metallic noise, the car lurched to a stop. Monir looked out his window, his spirits sinking. This wasn't an ordinary pothole—more like a circular ditch in the middle of the road. Monir feared the worst. Sure enough, the left side of the car knelt in the hole, defeated.

Staying calm, Monir got out and assessed the damage. The tire was flat, pressed against the front edge of the pothole.

A bird chirped in the distance. Monir interpreted it as a taunt and a stark reminder he was stuck in the middle of nowhere.

Against all hope he checked his phone. No service. He looked down the road he had come from, hoping for a rescue. *Who am I kidding?* he thought. *It could be days before another car appears.*

The afternoon had been a disappointment all around. Monir had woken up groggy and slightly disoriented from his nap to find out he had slept through his alarm. The sun was already starting to sink below the hills in the distance. Even so, wanting to make the most of the remaining hours of sunlight, he decided to venture out to the quarry.

Monir had driven his rental down the narrow streets of Agios Mamas to the main road. He took a left and drove along the winding and steadily ascending two-lane street to a T-intersection in Trimiklini. He turned right onto the main Limassol-Troodos road, then hung another right about a kilometer ahead, where a sign pointed toward Amiantos.

Upon reaching the picturesque village situated just a few kilometers from the quarry itself, he'd stopped at a local

71

coffee shop. Monir bought a bottle of water and a Snickers bar, then asked one of the locals who was sitting at a nearby table if he was on track for the quarry. That's when the trouble started.

One of the men—the only one who spoke understandable English—pushed Monir's map aside. "My friend, no good this. I show you best way." He faced the street and pointed north. "This way. Then left. Then right at school and left next. And after, you go straight…straight to quarry."

Monir looked down at his map and then back at the man with a puzzled expression on his face. Before he could say a word, the two other men started arguing in Greek with the first man. They were obviously not in agreement about the route he was suggesting.

One of them tried to tell Monir a better way, but the language barrier got the best of him. The third man jumped in, speaking solely in Greek and utilizing hand motions to indicate turns and straightaways.

Monir left the coffee shop confused. He decided to believe the first man about the uselessness of his map and tried to follow the man's instructions. Getting lost in the village almost immediately, he wound up at an old woman's driveway. Though friendly, she was of no help. He backed up and tried a few turns, which eventually got him to the school. A few turns later, Monir found his way to a long dirt road that did indeed lead to the quarry but emptied into a clearing whose road clearly hadn't been repaired in years. It was there that Monir's car was defeated by the mother of all potholes.

He looked down at his watch, then at the mountains ahead. The sun was only inches above the most distant peak in sight. It would be dark within the hour. A loud curse left his lips and echoed against the asbestos cliffs up ahead.

He heard the strange sound long before he saw it, but he couldn't make out what it was—understandably, as donkeys weren't used for transportation in any of the places Monir had lived.

He first saw the dark gray animal and its rider when they passed through the narrow space between two thickets, about a hundred meters from the road. Monir watched the unlikely duo, dumbfounded. His need for help prevailed over his amazement, so he yelled out.

"Hello!" He timidly waved a hand.

The old man riding the donkey seemed as rugged as the terrain. His wrinkled face, as well as his arms and hands, had certainly been exposed to inordinate amounts of sunlight, leaving the man with a permanent tan. The front rim of a well-worn straw boater hat cast a shadow over the man's eyes and down to the brim of his nose. His countenance was serious and concerned.

He did not respond to Monir's greeting. Instead, the man shot one swift glance at him before fixing his gaze on the car. He directed the donkey right to it, mumbling in Greek intermittently.

Dismounting a few meters away from the disabled vehicle, the man got on his hands and knees to get a better look at the wheel where the car had knelt in the ditch. He looked at it from several angles, grunting each time he moved his body lower toward the ground.

The man looked up at Monir, flattened his palms, and chopped the air, spreading his arms left and right. "Finish!"

"Yes...I was heading to the quarry...fell in the hole and..."

"Finish." More Greek followed the man's irrevocable verdict on the car. Asking if he spoke English was obviously out of the question, so Monir didn't bother.

"*Ela...file mou...ela.* Come...my friend...come."

Monir could see his eyes. They were a steely light blue. He saw great strength and decisiveness in them. A hint of impatience, but also compassion. Monir joined him by the donkey. He had no other choice.

What happened next was uncomfortable on several counts. The man insisted that Monir ride the donkey while he walked alongside them. It was the first time Monir had sat on the back of an animal, and the path was anything but flat. He tried to convince the man that he was happy to walk as well, but to no avail. The awkward trio carried on that way, all the way back to the village where Monir's troubles had begun.

By the time Monir and his rescuer entered Amiantos's paved roads, dusk had given way to the dark of night. People were in their homes. The streetlights were emitting their orange glow. Children's voices resounded through an open window. An elderly couple sat on their front porch, munching on sunflower seeds. Down the road, closer to the village center, the coffee shop regulars were seated inside and out. Along with the frequent sound of dice striking the wooden *tavli* board, loud men's voices filled the air with politics and sports commentary. Some sipped coffee; others smoked; a few were glued to the mounted TV in the corner.

Things got much quieter after the old man directed his donkey to take a right turn and then a left down a cobblestone alley. The donkey's hooves against the stones prevailed over all other early evening village sounds. It had to be the heart of the old village, thought Monir.

The old man, who had managed to teach Monir his name—Vangelis—mumbled to himself or his mule most of the way. Monir had stayed quiet.

At his house, Vangelis reunited with his wife and had a short conversation, both of them frequently nodding in the direction of the man whom their donkey had just transported to their yard. Their conversation, which was obviously about him, certainly did not help Monir with the awkwardness of the whole episode.

Obeying Vangelis's hand gestures, Monir followed the woman inside. The old man secured the donkey in a stall next to the house and joined them. His wife picked up the phone and dialed a number.

"OK," said the old man, nodding reassuringly. "Stalo. She come."

Vangelis's wife, who introduced herself to Monir as Evanthia, brought a pot of black-eyed peas to the table along with a plate of sliced tomatoes and cucumbers glazed with olive oil. A loaf of warm bread sat on a square wooden cutting board. *The old man must have fashioned that himself,* Monir thought.

His hosts bowed their heads briefly and then looked up at him. He saw from their faces that they would not begin unless he dug into the food first. He did.

They were almost finished eating when there was a knock at the door. A woman entered before anyone at the table could respond. She was very attractive, with long black hair and bright eyes.

"Good evening," she said, smiling. "My name is Stalo. My parents here informed me of your car problem. They called for me because...well, the language problem, of course."

Monir was on his feet right away, his hand extended. "Pleased to meet you. Thank you. I'm very grateful to your father for helping me. And to both your parents for their warm hospitality."

She gave him a firm handshake and sat next to her mother at the table. She murmured a few words in Greek to her parents while her eyes remained fastened on Monir's. "Where do you live, Mr....?"

"Monir. Monir Young. Agios Mamas is my place. Down...that way, I think."

He looked at the wall his finger was pointing to, then hesitantly back at her. Knowing nods from the parents upon his mention of the nearby village.

"And...it's Monir, just Monir. No title necessary." He was nervous, and everyone could tell.

More Greek followed between the three of them, and the only word Monir could make out was "Americanos."

"You are American?"

"Sort of. Um...it's a long story. Yes, I guess you can say that. American."

"I see," said Stalo. "But your first name is not an American name, right?"

"That's part of the long story. No, it's not."

"OK, Mr. Monir. No problem."

More brief Greek exchanges among the Cypriots. They all seemed to be in agreement. Nods all around.

"I'll take you home. No problem." She nodded at her father, signaling that it was Vangelis's recommendation. "But Agios Mamas—it's that way." She pointed behind Monir and smiled.

Monir laughed, partly at his lack of directional sense and partly at the pleasant surprise Stalo was turning out to be. It wasn't just her beautiful features and captivating smile. She was poised, confident, secure. She was in control of the environment in her parent's home from the moment she walked through the door. Her voice seemed to command respect when she spoke, as though she, the house, and even the village had an old and deep connection between them.

Stalo drove her silver VW fast, slowing down only for the sharpest of bends in the road. She asked many questions, mostly about Monir's background. He answered candidly, for the most part, only withholding information about the true nature of his work. When she asked about his job, the term "business consultant" seemed sufficient, and Monir was relieved.

He managed to learn a few things about her as well. She had been born and raised in Amiantos, attending elementary and middle school in the village. Then, after receiving a scholarship to Larnaca's renowned American Academy, Stalo moved to the city, staying with an aunt until she completed her secondary education.

Stalo's grandfather had worked in the quarry his whole life. He initially bought a small home at Amiantos, the village that had been constructed to accommodate the families mining asbestos. Over time he was promoted to supervisory positions, which afforded him a better life financially. He later bought a few fields, all of which he left to his only daughter, Stalo's mother.

Stalo's father was a farmer from a neighboring village. He had tended his and Stalo's mother's orchards and vineyards from time they had married. Their lifelong savings, combined with the proceeds from several back-to-back record harvest years, made a way for Stalo to study graphic design in England. She was hired by a Limassol firm shortly after her return from London. She had held the same position ever since.

Monir listened to Stalo talk, captivated. Despite his very long day—beginning with the plane ride from Geneva and ending with his ride on a donkey—he was wide awake. He wondered for a moment why that was, but as he waved goodbye to the beautiful Amiantos woman who had driven him home, the answer seemed obvious.

6
THE CAUSE

November: Geneva

Karl Braun was looking over some monthly financial reports at his desk when the intercom buzzed.

"Yes, Margret," he said in German, leaning in the direction of his desk phone's speaker.

"Mr. Ahmadi is on the line for you, sir."

Braun raised one eyebrow and tilted his head slightly. Although Farrouk Ahmadi worked for Karl and CORE, the German boss had never shaken his slight fear of the Jordanian operative.

This might not be good, he thought. "Put him through."

A short pause on the line, then a click.

"Good afternoon, Farrouk. What a pleasant surprise!"

"Hello, Karl."

"I didn't expect to hear from you until later this week."

Farrouk was never one to exchange niceties on the phone. In fact, he disliked conversations altogether. Part of it stemmed from his introverted personality. But it was

81

predominantly due to Farrouk's training and operational experience, which had instilled in him the persona of the conversational minimalist.

At the age of 19, Farrouk left his hometown to escape the constants of Ma'an's unemployment, poverty, and political unrest. He joined the Salafi-Jihadist movement in 1995 and shipped out for training in Afghanistan. Within two years, Farrouk had stood out as an effective mujahedeen and a brilliant strategic thinker. In a 1998 letter to his younger brother, Farrouk intimated he was being mentored by Osama bin Laden himself.

During his time in Afghanistan, Farrouk was introduced to an architect, Mohamad Rajhi, who, for reasons still unknown to Farrouk, was highly favored among the scores of construction professionals employed by the Saudi Binladin Group, Osama bin Laden's family business. The Group had just signed a $26.6 billion contract with the Saudi government to build King Abdullah Economic City, and Rajhi had been flown in to meet with the Sheik.

Farrouk, who had been assigned to escort the architect back to the airport after the meeting, made quite an impression on Rajhi. They stayed in touch over the next few years as Farrouk returned to Jordan after bin Laden's death, in 2011, to join a Jihadist movement under Abu Muhammad al-Maqdisi. Farrouk eventually distinguished himself enough to catch the notice of a new Islamist militant group that was making headlines worldwide for its brutal treatment of prisoners. The group called itself the Islamic State of Iraq and Syria, or ISIS. For a few months, Farrouk temporarily relocated to Syria to assess the possibilities of serving Jihad by collaborating with ISIS leadership.

Through Rajhi, Farrouk had become acquainted with a vast network of Arab and Western businessmen, all of whom had managed to lay cultural, ideological, and religious differences aside for the sake of financial gain. Then, at a function hosted by partners in the King Abdullah project, Farrouk met Karl Braun.

Farrouk was a perfect fit for CORE. As a mujahedeen, he had learned a ruthlessness that made him formidable in the field. His growing international operational networks and his expertise in resource acquisition gave him presence and finesse. A year into their collaboration, Karl asked Farrouk to consider "better serving the jihadist cause" by accepting a seven-figure salary and relocating to Europe. More importantly for Farrouk's jihadist network, Karl promised a cut from "a near future project of immense proportions." Farrouk accepted. He chose Vienna as his base of operations and began to assemble a team for the project Karl referred to as "Lithium Island."

"We have a situation, Karl. Switch to a secure line and call me back."

Karl opened his briefcase and retrieved his Thuraya XT-PRO satellite phone. He was back on with Farrouk in moments.

"Here I am."

Farrouk continued without further greeting. "The Frenchman talked to Nadia about the wires he found at the quarry. He suspects the mountainside was blown off. He showed pictures of the wires to a colleague. They were looking into the matter together."

"Does Nadia know who that is? Have they talked to anyone else about this?"

"We don't know, but we're working on it."

"We don't like loose ends, Farrouk."

"I told you all along I did not like the idea of trailing the geologists to the quarry. We could have gotten in through back channels with the government. Your well-connected banker there—"

"We've been over this, Farrouk. Geological teams have been exploring that mountainous region for years. They already had the trust of the government. It was the fastest and safest way for us to get in, observe, and make sure the mineral was plentiful." Karl got up from his desk and walked across the room. "Remember, we were not the only group that needed proof of the project's potential profitability. Your brothers, in Syria, for one; your Saudi business friends—"

"Leave them out of this. Their involvement has always hinged on stealth and secrecy. Blowing things up—especially mountains—draws too much attention."

"So do videos of brutality. Massacres, beheadings, and need I mention the burning of that pilot? Best I recall, he was your countryman, wasn't he?" Braun smiled at the taunt.

"No ally of the United States is my countryman. And what you and your whole western world call brutality is simply what is necessary for the establishment of our caliphate."

"Your caliphate needs billions of dollars, and that's why this deal has to go through for you. Speaking of caliphates, aren't the Turks on the move for this deal, too? Their president has been identifying with Turkey's caliphates from times past. I read that he recently welcomed VIPs in his lavish palace, surrounded by guards wearing costumes from Turkish and Ottoman history. He's even taken steps to revive Ottoman-era language."

"And your point, Karl?"

"Seems to me, Farrouk, as though the establishment of any caliphate—yours or theirs—and the subsequent world domination you jihadists dream of depends on the contents of the same treasure chest. Well, I have the key. It's Cyprus. Come to think of it, even the shape of the island resembles a key. There's your visual illustration for the day, Mr. Ahmadi. So for the good of *my* cause, you had better make sure your team in Cyprus knows what they're doing."

"I see."

"And do me a favor. Stick to secure mobile phones. Don't ever call my personal line in the office again."

* * *

Langley, Virginia, USA

When the CIA director had opened the lithium case in October and divvied up assignments, John Harden was given the task of gathering intelligence. He was told to start on the island of Cyprus itself and follow any leads to their sources, wherever they might be. Harden was chosen for two reasons: He always got the job done, and he had the best connections to the world of hackers.

Two days after the meeting, Harden made contact with an old friend, a U.S.-born Indian field agent who went by the name of Chandy. Harden didn't know where his pal would be when he called him. He didn't even ask, because it never mattered. As long as Chandy had a phone and an internet connection, the man could work from anywhere.

"We need you to get tabs on some people over in Cyprus, Chandy. Most likely a multiethnic team that's working for a European company we've had our eyes on for years."

"Is that CORE?"

"So you know about them?"

"This team you speak of—are they professionals?"

"Looks like it."

"Government or private?"

"Private, we think."

"What's the objective?"

Harden filled in his colleague about the lithium discovery in Cyprus, as well as the potential conspiratorial scenario that was suggested by the explosives at the quarry.

"I'd start with the government, Chandy. When there's big money to be had, there are big deals to be made. If our sources are accurate about the lithium quantities, the government will undoubtedly be involved. And so will everyone trying to make a buck on the side."

Chandy started to quote a favorite statement of one of the Agency's former directors. "Corruption marks the trail…"

John joined in mid-sentence. "…to the deepest part of the forest."

"Exactly!"

"Let me make some calls."

"Thanks. And Chandy, I'm also sending in a team from Munich."

"The Blakes?"

"Is there anything you *don't* know?"

"I like to stay informed. I'll be in touch soon."

Chandy made calls to three secure phones in India. Two were in Mumbai, one was in Bangalore. He employed a small team of people, none of whom had ever met the others. They would not be packing suitcases, and they would not be boarding flights. None would set foot on Cypriot shores. They would sit at home or in internet cafés, tapping away at their laptops. And within a week or so, they would have their target.

*　　*　　*

It was the top story in the evening news and the headline in all Cypriot papers the next morning:

HISTORIC AGREEMENT BETWEEN RUSSIA AND CYPRUS

After three days of talks in Moscow, the Russian president and his Cypriot counterpart signed an agreement whereby Russian military ships would be granted access to Cypriot ports. Russian ships and warplanes would also be allowed to use airports and seaports in humanitarian crises. In return, Russia restructured the $2.5 billion euro loan to Cyprus it had signed in 2011. The annual interest rate was reduced from 4.5% to 2.5%, and the redemption period was extended to 2021.

The Russian leader told journalists he was pleased with the agreement because such military cooperation would enable Russia to "join other nations in the fight against terrorism and piracy in the region."

Vasily and Darya Avdeyev were employed by the Foreign Intelligence Service of the Russian Federation (SVR RF). Semyon Entsky, the director of the SVR, had met with them in his office one Monday evening near the end of September. He had given them a thumb drive with all the necessary information for their upcoming mission. They would be heading to Cyprus, where they would be uniting with the two members of their team who had been sent there a few weeks earlier.

Earlier that morning, Entsky had met with the Russian president for his weekly Monday briefing. Entsky had presented him with information he had received from a department head with the Directorate PR, the SVR branch responsible for political intelligence in various countries of the world. A team of geologists had found lithium at an old asbestos quarry in the mountains of Cyprus. His agent Dimitry Kanadov had tracked the geologist's subsequent movements through one of his local assets, a Cypriot government official who had done work for Kanadov for about a decade.

"The quantities of the mineral are substantial, Mr. President."

The president reached into the top drawer of his desk, pulling out the recent *Moscow Times* piece about the Cyprus deal. Eyes back on the SVR director, the president asked, "Do you know why we had to pull $151 billion out of Cyprus last year?"

Entsky began to offer his answer, but the president interrupted him. "Theft insurance."

Though he was not entirely certain where his leader was going with that comment, the director knew better than to break the flow of the president's thoughts. He pursed his lips, frowned, and nodded.

"We sent $211 billion to Cyprus between 1994 and 2011, Semyon. The Europeans snatched $60 billion of our money to 'bail out' Cyprus from its 2012 banking debacle. Last year's capital outflows protect us from losing more. But I'm not here just to play defense!" He paused for a few seconds, then continued, his voice a bit lower than before.

"Assad's war forced us to evacuate civilian and military personnel from Tartus. We lost our base in Syria. No one's been willing to have us on their shores since then. But this…" The president held up the article. "This is our chance!"

"Indeed, Mr. President."

"This ensures we can establish a safe environment in which our money can grow again—in euros, not rubles. And it gives us the military foothold we so desperately need."

Entsky chuckled. "Under the noses of the Turks, the Americans, and the Europeans, too. They've stayed out of the matter, for the most part."

"Which brings us to my next point. Just like the Americans and the European Union don't care about Cyprus's ports or its banks, I don't care about the lithium. It's not for us to have…but I don't want them to get their hands on it either."

Entsky pondered the president's words for a moment. Then he placed his hand on the desk and nodded.

"Understood, Mr. President."

"Proper positioning is everything, Semyon. Cyprus could very well find itself in the center of a massive geopolitical storm in the years to come. Our military and our funds—and our citizens who live in Cyprus—will play a key role, if we have the right position. And that has to be our primary focus. Monitor everything, then make sure nothing comes of this lithium find—especially for the Turks and the Americans."

7

DAVIN VALOIS

June: Limassol, Cyprus

Stalo and Monir had exchanged phone numbers before she dropped him off at his place the night he'd been stranded at the quarry. She had also written down the number of a local towing company for his car.

Monir called her two days later. He told her that the car rental company had taken over the entire operation of getting the car out of the pothole and repairing it. Furthermore, they had provided Monir with a different vehicle.

"Well, I'm glad things worked out," Stalo said. It's nice that you called."

"I'm in your area. I've been sightseeing a bit. I thought maybe we could have coffee."

Sightseeing is partly true, Monir thought as he replayed some of the day's wanderings in his mind. Earlier in the morning, he had followed his map back to the quarry, this time taking the paved roads all the way to the entrance and going in from the front. He did not even look in the direction of the

93

Amiantos coffee shop when he passed by it, annoyed by the memory of the "help" he'd received there. He did wonder, however, where Stalo's parents' house was, as it had been dark the night Vangelis led Monir there on his donkey. He was also curious about where she lived. *Probably not far from her folks,* he thought.

Once in the quarry itself, Monir had driven as far as he could in the direction of the first location where the lithium had been found. A meter-high white wooden roadblock was positioned across the road, forbidding entry into the last 400-meter stretch to the site. A red sign hung in the middle of the fence. It bore several Greek words in all capitals and the words "NO ENTRY. STAY OUT" in English. Monir parked the car on the side of the road and walked past the roadblock.

He'd meandered around the lithium site for about an hour, taking notes and pictures. It was his first time seeing the mineral up close. He had, of course, spent hours researching it online.

Stalo's voice in his ear jolted him back to the present. "I'd love to have coffee," she said, "but...not here, not in this village. Too many busybodies."

"I understand. How about somewhere near the water? In Limassol. This evening, that is. Somewhere busy and lively— away from the busybodies."

"Colors!" Stalo said.

Monir was confused. "Colors?"

"It's the café in the Four Seasons. There's a nice deck by one of the pools. Very cosmopolitan. Oh, and the desserts—they have gold flakes on them! Yes?"

"Sold!" Monir chuckled at her excitement over the sweets. Colors it was.

It had been quite the day for him. He was satisfied with what he saw earlier that morning at the quarry. Things were definitely on track in terms of his mission. But he was positively intrigued by what stirred inside him inside every time he spoke to Stalo. Her presence, even over the phone, enthralled him. And he loved it.

The last rays of sunlight retreated beyond the watery horizon, leaving behind layers of radiant orange, pink, and yellow in the sky. Monir and Stalo sat on the corner of the Colors deck, only meters away from the lit-up pool of the Four Seasons. Though the restaurant was full of people and the poolside patio was busy, the two of them seemed oblivious to all the sights and sounds that surrounded them. They were engaged in a deep conversation that had begun about an hour earlier, up in the mountains, when Stalo had picked up Monir at his place.

She had asked him a series of questions about his recent arrival in Cyprus. What drew him to the island-nation? Why did he choose to stay at Agios Mamas? Why did he venture out to the Amiantos quarry on his first night in the country? Her tone was friendly, even playful at times, yet it was evident to Monir that Stalo had been doing some thinking since she'd met him at her parents' house.

Evading the truth had never been a problem for Monir, especially when lucrative contracts were on the line. He had done it with government leaders, bankers, legal teams, and even his own bosses in Geneva. He had never perceived his untruths to be lies—they were negotiating tools he deemed necessary for success. Once, while referring to the nebulous reasons he had given Bolivian emerald miners for being interested in their assets, Monir told a coworker that he hadn't lied. "I simply engineered the truth."

He had been engineering truths all the way down the mountain, but Stalo's instincts told her something was up. Just as they turned left onto the beachfront road that led to Colors, she asked a question that proved to be more of an ultimatum. "Monir, I have no right whatsoever to demand answers to my questions. And you have absolutely no obligation to respond to them. But it's important for me to know that when you talk to me, you are truthful. Is that too much to ask?"

After they placed their order for gelato and coffee, Monir apologized for his evasiveness. "Maybe it's because of the nature of my work and my guardedness with someone I just met."

He told Stalo about his job as chief negotiator for a Geneva-based company that specialized in commodities. Next, using broad strokes, he painted the picture regarding the lithium find. He never named the mineral, but he did reveal that the original discovery had been made at the quarry that Stalo's village had been named after, Amiantos. She assumed it was a new vein of asbestos and left it at that, not asking for any clarification.

"So, I'm here because my company sent me to negotiate a deal with your government."

Up until that point, Stalo's eyes had shown her satisfaction with Monir's newfound forthrightness. But the moment he mentioned his company's intentions to secure a deal, Stalo's, dark brown eyes looked down at the table.

"What's the matter? I'm telling you the truth."

"I know, and I appreciate it. It's just that…well, I know where all this is leading."

"What do you mean?"

Her voice quivered with disappointment. "The *deal*. Our mineral. Your company. Our government. It's the story of my country, going back thousands of years. We've always had valuable natural resources here—iron, copper, silver, even lumber at one point. First, it was foreign invaders who exploited us—the Romans, the Venetians, the British, the Turks. Now it's multinational corporations like yours."

Monir was starting to understand. He had definitely touched a nerve. He knew she wasn't finished yet, so he remained quiet.

"It's not your fault," she continued. "It's ours. Our own shortsightedness, along with greed and corruption, have done more damage than conquerors' swords and rifles. And for what? We sell out to the highest bidder, then squander the money. And now, more than ever, we're left with nothing to show for it."

Stalo looked past Monir to some children who were playing in the shallow end of the hotel's pool. She seemed lost in thought for a moment, then mumbled, "But at least now I understand why Davin was up there with his team all that time."

"Who?" Monir said sharply.

"Who what?"

"The Frenchman. You just mentioned him. What was the name?"

"Davin. Davin Valois. I talked to him a couple of times. Nice guy. He was up at the village with a team of scientists for weeks. They went to the quarry almost every morning.

Then he was gone. The others stayed a while longer, but Davin was—"

Monir was on his feet before she could finish her sentence. "Where's the waiter? We have to go. I have to get back to my place."

"Now?"

"Yes, right now!"

"Well, that's weird, don't you think? We just got here." She looked down at her watch. Monir had already called for the bill and was pulling cash out of his wallet to pay. "Plus, this is the worst time to head back up the mountain."

"What? Why? Listen, I'm really sorry. I know we're having a good time, and I do love being here with you. But what you said, the French guy, I have to look into something."

"Still makes no sense to me. And I'm telling you, this is bad timing, but maybe we'll get lucky."

"Get lucky? What are you talking about?"

"The garbage trucks. A whole fleet of them, up around Alassa. They all come out around this time and head up toward the mountain villages. Believe me, you don't want to be stuck behind them around those turns, where you can't pass."

Monir ran his hand through his hair. Stalo thought she was talking some sense into him, that he was contemplating the chance of encountering the garbage truck convoy on their way home. He wasn't. Monir's mind was racing with questions about the implications of Stalo's geologist being the same Davin Valois from his Vienna flight to Geneva back in January.

Monir and Stalo's ride back was uneventful—they never encountered the garbage trucks that night—but things became very awkward as the two of them reverted back to small talk about travel, politics, and weather patterns. The events that had unfolded back at Colors had certainly derailed the date.

All things considered, though, in the back of his mind, Monir was glad that he and Stalo were parting on good terms and had agreed to talk soon. Even so, from the moment he entered his house until sleep overtook him in the pre-dawn hours of the next day, Monir was intensely focused on the task of finding information about Davin Valois.

Monir's online search for the Frenchman's name revealed that "Davin" and "Valois" were town names in the American states of West Virginia and New York, respectively. Scrolling down, he also found write-ups about individuals whose names were either Davin or Valois but not both. Then, near the bottom of the page, Monir's concerns were validated:

The French citizen found dead in the Schwechat airport's long-term car park has been identified as 45-year-old **Davin Valois**...

Monir searched through the online archives of the Vienna newspapers and discovered two other blurbs about the incident. The deceased was a tourist who had flown in from Cyprus a few days earlier. He had been found in a silver Mercedes. The cause of death was a bullet wound in the head. The weapon was not found. Foul play was suspected. An investigation had turned up nothing and remained open.

After exhausting all possible online research venues, Monir looked into the dates on which the various write-ups had been published. All of them had been posted near the end of January—closely matching the date on which Monir had taken and filed away pictures of a mysterious couple on his flight to Geneva. This had to be the same Davin Valois.

Monir lay on his bed with two pillows propped under his head, his eyes wandered around the ceiling. His mind was racing, processing everything he had seen, heard, and read about Davin Valois. He formulated questions, some of which he even said aloud to the light fixture above him.

What was Davin Valois's connection to the lithium discovery? Was his death related to the mineral? Were any members of Davin's team still around? Who shot him? Was it a mugging, or was it a premeditated assassination?

A wave of adrenaline hit Monir's gut as he answered the last question for himself. *Thugs don't hit airport long-term parkers,* he thought. *And they certainly leave clues behind.* All the evidence pointed to the work of professionals. *But why was a tourist parking long term?*

Monir's eyelids were beginning to yield to his sleepiness. He lay still on top of the bed, his breathing already slowing down, but his mind kept going. *I have to talk to Stalo about all this…and I should email Karl…Farrouk lives in Vienna. Maybe he knows something…or perhaps the lithium find is not at all a part of this and I should just move on.*

The light stayed on, but it didn't bother him in the least. By the time sleep had taken over Monir, the distant rays of dawn were signaling the start of a new day in Cyprus.

8
EYES AND EARS

December: Washington, D.C., USA

John Harden was pleased to see Chandy's name on the screen of the secure phone that was buzzing on his kitchen counter. He quickly swallowed the piece of apricot jam–covered toast he had just bitten off and pressed the talk button.

"Give me the good news, Chandy."

"Nothing from CORE's network as of yet. The few leads we thought we had led nowhere. Their firewalls are hard to penetrate; top notch encryption, too."

"How about the Cyprus side of things?"

"Better luck there. The email server of the Ministry of the Interior gave us a good idea of how the whole lithium thing got started."

Chandy briefed Harden about the geological team from Cambridge, led by Davin Valois. First, the application for exploration rights; then, the invitation by the ministry; followed by all lithium-related correspondence between

Valois, Cambridge, and the ministry after the mineral was discovered.

"Do you have tabs on the scientists?"

"Not yet. That's why I'm calling. Your Munich couple, the Blakes—"

"Tyson and Cynthia are in position. They've checked out the site where the lithium was initially found, and they've confirmed there's loads of the stuff in those mountains. They've located the geological team and rented a condo near them. They're also keeping an eye on other players."

"Russians?"

"Yup, primarily."

"Who else?"

"Maybe the Brits. You know they're always watching and listening." Harden was referring to one of Great Britain's two spying stations. They'd retained two military bases on Cyprus since the island's independence from British rule in 1959. Both bases contributed significantly to the spying operations of the Global Communications Headquarters.

"What about the Turks up north?"

"A little fuss at the beginning, Tyson said. Quiet now. The usual diplomatic dance with the Cypriots. Going nowhere, I'd say."

"Any sighting of CORE activity?"

"Not sure. Blakes just got there recently—it'll take more time. What do you need from them?"

"I have to get a read on that Valois fellow. Bugs on his phone, computer, car, condo, and any place he frequents."

"Sure thing. It's their specialty."

"Have the Blakes send everything to me and I'll pass it along to my people."

"Can they tap the Russians, too, while they're at it?"

"If it's a state-run operation, forget about it. Remember how the SVR brought in Chinese cyber-geniuses to update their systems 10 years ago? No way into that fortress. But maybe it's a private corporation."

"Fat chance. Ultimately, everything is state-run in Russia, regardless of the label."

* * *

As they had been instructed by Harden, Tyson and Cynthia Blake managed to open up several windows into Davin's life in less than a week. Working from surveillance the Blakes had conducted on the geologists, Tyson knew when the bungalows were vacant every day.

He broke into Davin's place shortly after the SUVs had pulled out. Tyson placed listening devices in the living room, the hallway, and the Frenchman's bedroom.

Cynthia worked alone as well to bug Davin's rental car. It was a two-step process. First, she used a different embassy vehicle—not the green Pajero—to follow Davin's team from Amiantos all the way to the outskirts of Kyperounta Village, where the GEOBOR drilling was taking place at the end of a rugged dirt trail about 100 meters from the main road. In order to avoid the possibility of breaking an axle or getting stuck in the mud after it rained, the team had been parking their SUVs along the side of the road. When the RAV4s pulled aside to park that morning, Cynthia went past them about a kilometer and parked in the woods.

She took out her backpack and walking stick and hiked back to the spot where the scientists had left their rentals. As she walked by Davin's rental, Cynthia bent down to tie her shoe. She looked around, ascertained she was alone, and then placed a magnetic tracking device under the RAV4's frame.

She and Tyson followed the signal to Limassol the next evening, connecting with the car on the A1 highway between the Agios Athanasios and Yermasogia exits. They trailed Davin in their Pajero as he performed several small errands and wound up at an open parking field across from the renowned beachfront restaurant Fat Fish. To ensure that Valois did not see them, they left their car at a hotel up the road and doubled back. Once darkness had fully settled on the parking area, Cynthia stood watch while Tyson broke into Davin's vehicle and inserted a pin-like listening device into the upholstery right above the driver-side window. It took all of four minutes.

Tapping into Davin's computer was simple. They parked near the center of Amiantos and strolled by Davin's bungalow in the middle of the night. Opening their phones' Wi-Fi settings, they saw only one available network: Cambridge3714. Tyson took a small handheld device out of his pocket. Within a few minutes, the device had cracked the password for the Wi-Fi network. They were in. Davin Valois's internet activity was now monitored by the CIA.

*　　*　　*

Larnaca, Cyprus

Dimitry Kanadov's inside source had yet again turned up with information that was gold. The source went by the name Kontos—a nickname, he once told his Russian handler, that was given to him in the army because of his short stature.

Kontos had bribed a friend in the immigration office for printed records of the foreigners who had entered Cyprus through the Larnaca and Paphos airports over the last six months. Dimitry and the Avdeyevs went through the records several times. U.S. embassy employees Andrew Remington and Rene Fletcher were of particular interest, as they had arrived on November 20th and 23rd, respectively, and had not left yet. The Russian agents scanned the Americans' passport info into an email they sent back to their superiors. A small team of analysts matched the pictures to an SVR database and forwarded their findings to the director's office.

Semyon Entsky looked over the results and phoned Dimitry in Cyprus, getting straight to the point.

"Just like we thought: The Americans are in your backyard."

"We suspected as much."

"They came from the Munich station. A couple posing as unmarried embassy workers. We identified them as Tyson and Cythia Blake. You know what to do."

The call ended as abruptly as it had begun. Then Dimitry called the Avdeyevs.

As Nadia and her employers rightly predicted, now that Davin had started talking to her about his work, it wasn't taking long for her to extract all the information she needed.

Though Davin never mentioned the name of the colleague with whom he had shared his suspicions about the explosives, he told Nadia that his closest confidant on the team was an American. She passed on the information to the Watchers, who had an easy time picking out Doug from the rest of Davin's geologists: He was the only one speaking with an American accent when the group sat down at Makris Family Restaurant near Platres for a late lunch one Friday afternoon.

Dietrich and Yury, who had been monitoring the team's activities all morning, entered the restaurant 10 minutes after the geologists arrived. Davin was not with them, as he was in Nicosia, briefing government officials about the GEOBOR's findings on the eastern slopes of Troodos Mountain.

The Watchers sat within earshot of the team and listened. They had been instructed to find the American in the group. The moment Doug directed a comment about the tenderness of the chicken across the table to Gloria, the Watchers looked at each other. When their own meals arrived, a smiling Yury pulled out his phone and pretended he was taking pictures of his lamb chops. He kept his finger long enough on the screen to snap about a dozen shots of his meal. Then, moving the camera lens slightly upward, finger still on the button, he photographed the American. Doug had been spotted and tagged.

The plan was to keep an eye on Doug's whereabouts when he was off work and possibly to get a look into his communications by hacking into his computer. At the appropriate moment, the Watchers would abduct Doug and question him about what he knew.

"You'll get him talking in no time," Farrouk had stated toward the end of his recent conference call with Dietrich, Yury, and Nadia. "At the same time, we'll be taking care of the Frenchman in Vienna. No mistakes. No loose ends." A short pause on the line and then he continued. "Nadia, you'll be receiving instructions about Vienna very soon."

*   *   *

Limassol, Cyprus

The white Lexus SUV had been idling on the curb beneath the Watchers' apartment complex for some time. Farrouk's last words had just come through the vehicle's speakers. The man behind the driver turned to the woman who was sitting next to him. They nodded to each other without saying a word. She bent her head slightly forward, he responded with a long blink of his eyes, then he tapped the driver on the shoulder. Within seconds the Lexus was cruising along the beachfront road. The man pulled out his secure phone, tapped on the screen, and held the device between him and the woman.

"Hello," said a deep male voice.

"Everyone is in position."

"Like we thought?"

"Yes. The usual suspects, plus the wolves. And they're about to strike."

"We'll have instructions for you shortly. Be careful out there. Shalom."

9

INSIDERS

June: Nicosia, Cyprus

Café Anamnisis was located just a few blocks away from the wall. The imposing stone barricade that had once constituted the outermost rampart of Lefkosia—renamed Nicosia under Latin rule in the eighteenth century—had withstood the hardship of wars and the trends of modernity. Standing 20 meters above the busy streets of Cyprus's divided capital city, the wall formed the boundary between the Cypriot and Turkish sides.

If they had turned toward it, the two men would have seen a setting so characteristic for many spots along the 180-km-long Turkish–Greek demarcation line. Cypriot barracks on the south side of the wall, an elevated Turkish military guard post on the north side. Between them, a demilitarized zone occupied by UN peacekeeping forces.

The older man had arrived first and had chosen a table on the upper terrace of the restaurant. He ordered coffee and fidgeted with his phone. His guest arrived shortly, expressing apologies for the delay. He said traffic was horrendous due to construction, plus he had to park far, as there were no vacant spots by the restaurant. He asked the waitress for a frappé and took a seat.

The two men engaged in small talk for a few minutes, discussing mostly the weather and the latest news from the world of soccer. A recent FIFA Champions League drawing had just come out, whereby the local champions, Apoel, would be contending against FC Barcelona in the coming months.

"Did you hear the news about Apoel and—"

He was cut off mid-question. "No chance, my dear Angelos, no chance," the older man exclaimed between sips of his coffee. Angelos did not respond. He took off his Ray-Ban shades and laid them on the table. Then he turned and faced the barricaded border. The Cypriot, UN, and Turkish flags were all fluttering in the steady wind. The heat was already creating a mirage-like effect on the barren fields between the restaurant and the wall.

Angelos didn't actually have an opinion about the upcoming game. He had only tried to bring up the subject because it was a cultural norm to ease into the matters at hand through light conversation. And by his posture, the younger man was making it clear that soccer commentary was over and they were about to shift into business.

Awkwardly, the older man lowered his voice and offered the last word. "No chance against Barcelona. Not here, and definitely not in Spain. Messi is just unstoppable these days."

"Our contact is here, Mr. Sophroniou," Angelos said coolly. He always addressed the man by his last name, out of respect for both his age and position.

The 69-year-old Orestis Sophroniou had been the longtime director of Cyprus's Mining Department of the Ministry of Agriculture and Natural Resources. His 38 years of service in that post had been very fruitful. Under Sophroniou's leadership the department had received numerous government awards, grants, and favorable nods from foreign delegations, most notably the endorsement of the Environment Directorate-General of the European Commission. As a result of his success and seniority, Sophroniou had become widely respected in government circles. He was quiet, calculating, and strategic, always keeping a low profile publicly while nurturing the right friendships and alliances in private. As one of the government's oldest active statesmen, Sophroniou was in the rare category of leaders who could boast of having numerous valuable allies and few enemies.

The contact Angelos referred to was CORE's negotiator, Monir Young. Sophroniou had never met or even heard of Monir; however, he was well acquainted with the company's

CEO, Karl Braun. The two men had been introduced by Giannis Theodorou in the mid-'90s. They had only met in person once, in Limassol, during one of Karl's money-stashing trips to the bank, but they had hit it off well. They'd spoken generally about working together in the future, but they hadn't stayed in touch afterward.

Until 2008, that is. Banks and other financial institutions were collapsing in the U.S., the UK, and numerous European nations. The Dow Jones and all economies dependent on the New York Stock Exchange were suffering the effects of catastrophic sellouts. China was rising, but other Asian economies, particularly Japan's, were a mess, due to a long-lasting deflation. And yet oil prices were skyrocketing, indicating that commodities might end up on an upturn for the long haul.

Braun saw his opportunity and began to explore the possibilities for expansion into new markets. Cyprus was high up on his list. First, he called Theodorou to inquire about the potential corruptibility of the nation's mining department director. "The man you introduced me to a few years back—Orestis, I believe was his name—you think he'd be interested in working with us?"

The banker assured Braun of Sophroniou's cooperation by citing a number of favors the man had done for him over the years, "all of which were well compensated, of course."

116

That was music to Karl's ears. He quickly arranged a conference call for the three men. At first, the talk revolved around digging for gold on the Troodos Mountain Range. Orestis Sophroniou said he was interested, but he did not believe there was much gold to be had in Cyprus. Companies from Australia and Canada had already done extensive digging on a smaller range northwest of Nicosia, with little success.

He then brought up an academic paper that had been published by a professor friend of his in the 1980s. The man, a geologist from Scotland, had been invited to offer a series of lectures at the University of Cyprus. Sophroniou said the professor's thesis was drawing from the island's geological history to suggest there were substantial mineral deposits in the largest mountain ranges of Troodos and Pentadaktylos.

Karl Braun wasted no time. With Sophroniou's full assent, he dispatched a small team of CORE scientists to investigate. Over the next few years, while posing as fossil hunters and amateur rock enthusiasts, the team studied rock formations over many of the island's mountainous regions. Their conclusions, after half a dozen reconnaissance expeditions, concurred with those of the Scottish professor. High concentrations of marketable minerals lay deep beneath the roots of Cyprus's majestic pines and the volcanic remnants upon which they had grown.

But what minerals were they talking about, and in what quantities? The answers to those questions could only come if more extensive studies were performed, and those kinds of explorations would require blasting. Unfortunately, obtaining the permits necessary for legal blasting would take time and money—and in the meantime, someone besides CORE might put up a fight for the minerals. During one of his discussions with Sophroniou in 2012, Braun had explained that CORE was well equipped to execute the necessary blasts now, but his team would have to operate under a better cover than before.

Enter the French professor from Cambridge, Davin Valois, and his application to study rock formations at the old Amiantos quarry.

"This geological expedition is the ultimate Trojan Horse for you, my friend," Sophroniou had told Braun after receiving Valois's request. "We just have to time the explosions so that the Cambridge team can 'discover' whatever your blasts expose."

Karl loved it. He suggested that the blasting take place during a time of heavy rainfall. "We have the technology to cause explosions that are relatively quiet. Anyone who hears them during a rainstorm will attribute the sound to thunder and the blast's impact to erosion." It was a brilliant plan,

Sophroniou had said, and thus the Cypriot head of mining proceeded to strike a deal with the German CEO.

Upon completion of the first phase—ending with the blasting of a slope at Amiantos quarry—Sophroniou would receive 50,000 euros in a Bulgarian account. Then, for the second phase, the Cypriot official would be awarded half a million euros in return for leveraging relationships within the government. Sophroniou would oil all the wheels on his side of the table and would set up a deal between CORE and the Cyprus government for the exploitation of whatever mineral Braun's blasts exposed. Giannis Theodorou was also in on the agreement, as he would work with Sophroniou on the home front to recruit one more local asset: a man who would be the group's local eyes and ears once the minerals were found.

That man was Angelos Mavros, a mid-level officer in the mining department of the Ministry of Agriculture and Natural Resources. He had been a high-school classmate of Theodorou. The two men had also enlisted together in the infantry during their time of conscription on the island. They were both stationed at a remote outpost outside the village of Tylliria. During the endless hours of patrols and guard duty, Giannis and Angelos spoke extensively and realized they had similar frustrations with the status quo, as well as near-identical aspirations for the future.

They went their separate ways after the army, Theodorou to the United States for a finance degree, Mavros to England for accounting. The two friends reconnected about a decade later and picked up where they had left off during their military years. Always the recruiter of talent for "special extracurricular projects," as the banker had once put it to Karl Braun, Theodorou was convinced that his smart, ambitious, and socially disillusioned friend would be a perfect candidate for the mineral job.

Once the lithium was "discovered" in September, and Cambridge obtained permission to bring in the GEOBOR for further drilling, Sophroniou found the perfect opportunity to get Mavros involved.

Sophroniou convinced Mavros's supervisor, just an elevator ride down to the second level of the same building, that someone from that office had to be assigned to the geologists in order to ensure the preservation of the topography, and especially the 10 different species of pine trees that grew on the Troodos Range. Over a private lunch he hosted, Sophroniou mentioned to his colleague that he had heard great things about Mavros and that he'd like him to be considered for the job.

It worked. Mavros was given the task of accompanying the Cambridge geologists to the various drill sites; thus, from the moment Davin Valois began to venture beyond the Amiantos quarry with his GEOBOR, the Cypriot collaborators and Karl Braun's Watchers had an inside track to the lithium find.

*　　*　　*

"Have you talked to him?" Sophroniou asked.

"Not yet," Mavros replied. "He's taking a few days to acclimate. Some of Braun's people said he was traipsing around the quarry the other day."

"Let him be. We still need some time to set up things on our end. Plus, the president's been out of town, and so has my liaison to him, his chief of staff." It was Sophroniou's turn to cast a look in the direction of the demarcation wall. He sighed deeply and narrowed his eyes before leveling them on his young accomplice.

"I'm not concerned about the salesman Braun sent. It's the Frenchman I'm worried about. What on earth happened to him in Vienna? Who killed him? Why?"

Angelos didn't even blink. "You need to stop poking into matters that don't concern us, sir."

"Oh they concern us, all right!" The senior official looked around to make sure no one was close enough to hear him. He lowered his voice and explained. "Karl said the man was on to us about the blasts. He may have talked to people. Do you understand the implications of that?"

Angelos opened his mouth to speak, but Sophroniou wasn't done yet.

"No one knows the German; he and his men can pull out and disappear at any moment. You and I live here. We have families. We have jobs. This is our country!"

Angelos leaned forward, both hands motioning as though he was slowing down cars on the road. "Please, Mr. Sophroniou, relax. Everything is under control." He paused momentarily to look around the premises, ensuring their privacy. "The Frenchman is out, and no one has come forth with anything that is alarming to us. Valois was killed by a thug who wanted his wallet—period. His team went back to Cambridge, and we carry on. For God's sake, relax!"

Sophroniou bowed his head. "OK. When do you meet with Karl's man—what was his name, again?"

"Young. Monir Young. I'll meet with him tomorrow or the next day. I'll walk him through everything. Hopefully, the president gets back on Tuesday, as expected, and we can move things along."

Sophroniou reached across the table and tapped Angelos on the forearm. Fear was still lingering around in his eyes. "Be careful out there. We have way too much to lose if this goes wrong."

Angelos was on his feet momentarily, repositioning the Ray-Bans over his nose. "Everything will work out. The only thing *wrong* here is that I have to walk all the way down the street to my car in this heat." He waved a curt goodbye and walked away from the table.

"Remember, Apoel doesn't have a chance against Barcelona," Sophroniou yelled as Mavros was passing through the arched door to the outer stairwell. "You mark my words." He chuckled to himself nervously. If only he could be as certain about the outcome of their dealings as he was about the upcoming Champions League game. He had a bad feeling about it all, and Mavros had not done much to brighten his outlook.

10
MYRA KORTELLI

Myra's phone started buzzing at 6:15 on Sunday morning. She was expecting the call a bit later in the day, so it took her by surprise. Groggy, she reached for the device on her nightstand and looked at the screen. Almost instantly she was wide awake. She ended the vibrations of the handheld device by answering the call, whispered "One moment" in English, draped the hotel bathrobe over her shoulders, and quickly exited the room.

Just then, Davin opened his eyes and turned his head toward her side of the bed. Myra was already gone. Her calm, low tones, coming faintly from the sitting area of their suite, assured Davin that it was not an alarming call. He went back to sleep.

The caller sounded hoarse. He spoke in Russian slowly, decisively.

"Next weekend. Vienna—according to the plan. Follow the instructions you'll be receiving from us in the next day or two."

"Yes. See you soon," Myra replied. She turned off the phone, reentered her room and bed, and snuggled up to Davin.

"Who was it, Myra?" he said sleepily.

"Fashion show–related. I'll tell you over breakfast."

They were spending the weekend at yet another magnificent Cypriot hotel. Blu Mirage was located just north of the island's westernmost city, Paphos. Davin and Myra had occupied one of the suites on the tenth floor for two days. Luxury extraordinaire: the finest in culinary delights, made to order by renowned chefs, and available through room service 24 hours a day. The latest in TV and movie entertainment on a massive built-in LED screen across from the plush, meter-high, king-sized bed. Exquisite furnishings and interior design that tastefully combined Greek traditional with cutting-edge modern. A spacious walk-in shower off the master bedroom, its walls featuring soothingly cascading waters atop mosaic depictions of Greek mythological characters. A small private patio through the exterior double doors, complete with its own mini–hanging gardens and an elevated Jacuzzi.

"You don't just get a nice view from here," Davin had remarked on the first night, immersed in 42-degree water to his neck and looking over the tub's edge toward the moonlit Mediterranean waters. "It feels like we're sitting right on top of the ocean."

"Aren't you glad you took the time away from your rocks?" Myra asked while handing Davin a glass of wine.

One of the things Davin loved about his job was that no matter how hard he and his team worked on the mountains during the week, their weekends were generally free, primarily because Angelos Mavros, the government official assigned to Davin's crew, only worked Monday through Friday.

"Mmm. Well, it wasn't easy. We still have so much to do, weekend or not. But it's definitely proving to be worth it."

Having sequestered themselves in the suite long enough to enjoy most of the room's amenities, and to enjoy each other, the couple opted to have breakfast at one of the hotel's restaurants. It was at Sirena's, located next to a large oval-shaped pool on the lower level, that Myra spoke about the subject of her early-morning phone call.

"My friend Simo works for Armani in New York. He got mixed up on the time zones, thought it was evening in Cyprus."

Over eggs, perfectly grilled halloumi, and an exquisite selection of breads and Greek olives, Myra laid out the latest tale she had weaved. Due to a colleague's sudden illness, Simo was short a fashion consultant for the huge Vienna show that was scheduled for the upcoming weekend. He needed Myra's help. Armani would fly her and anyone she might want to bring along to Vienna, and they would compensate her very generously if she would contribute her expertise for the show.

"I'd love it if you came with me," she said. "It should be really fun—Vienna!"

"I just have to shift a couple of meetings around, but I think I can do it." He picked up a kalamata olive and fed it to her across the table. "Should be fun, indeed!"

They checked out of the hotel at eleven o'clock and spent the afternoon driving around the various historical sites in Paphos. They had coffee by the old port and then completed their weekend getaway by attending the opening of an art exhibit at the Byzantine Museum. After the modest opening ceremony and the tour of the exhibit, the couple drove to

Phuket Thai and Chinese Restaurant, famed for its dim sum. As expected, the meal was fabulous, and the conversation between them was spirited and lively.

If there was anything Myra had learned on the job, it was to keep her heart from forming a genuine emotional connection with a target. From her end, being physically attracted to the man was always part of the deal. If she didn't like him, Farrouk and his superiors would have to set the honey trap with someone else. But physical attraction was as far as Nadia would go. She would carefully guard herself from dangerous entanglements that could cloud her judgment by operating completely within the confines of her fabricated personality. "Myra Kortelli," and every made-up fact of her life, not only protected Nadia's true identity but also paved the way for her plans for the future.

Myra finished gathering her coat and purse and slid out of the booth. Davin followed her initiative from across the table. He paid the tab and then escorted Myra out the door and toward his car. Just as they were about to part to enter the vehicle, Myra took Davin's hand in hers. Then she gently tugged on his shirt at the forearm, pulling him toward her. Her fingers interlocked with a tuft of his brown hair as she connected for a long kiss.

"Mmmf!" He was unable to get any words out before she landed her next kiss. She was completely in control, as she had been all weekend; as she had been, in fact, from the moment he first laid eyes on her.

"To be continued in Vienna. Our little escapades are going international now." She pecked him on the chin and walked past him to the passenger's side. Davin stood in place momentarily, dazed. He was expecting to have the time of his life in Vienna. He was partly correct.

An Armani show was indeed taking place in Vienna that weekend, but Myra Kortelli was by no means known to the organizers, much less sought after for her consulting services. Nor was she looking forward to another weekend of fine dining, shopping, and lovemaking with Davin. Yet, as she had done for more than three months, she would play the part of the romantic-getaway lover convincingly—and, if all went well, for the last time.

During the drive home the couple was silent for the first half hour. Davin was already shifting into work mode and was contemplating the drilling that had to take place near Kakopetria the next morning. He had to get test results and submit December's reports before leaving for Vienna. He'd leave Doug in charge of the team while he was gone. Reginald Wiley should be fine with it, so long as everything was progressing properly.

Myra had a completely different train of thought, one that started back home, in St. Petersburg. Nadia Dryovskaya, daughter to Nicolay and Malvina, had been raised in a modest home with two brothers and a sister. She graduated from school and moved to Europe to pursue her passion for international affairs.

After obtaining a degree in politics from Charles University, in Prague, she landed an internship at the UN in Geneva. She had always been bright and ambitious. She had a way with people, especially authority figures. Her striking features certainly helped, but it was her approach to interpersonal relationships that contributed the most to her fast ascent to places of influence.

It was during her internship that Nadia connected with one of Karl Braun's mercenaries, Yury Farnakov, through a friend at the UN. Beyond the fact that Yury was also Russian, Nadia was impressed with his lifestyle. They started dating, and during their outings Yury introduced Nadia to some of his coworkers. She was intrigued by them as well. Their nocturnal social lives projected every external benchmark of success: material possessions, class, and more. To discerning eyes, however, they also exhibited structure, discipline, focus, awareness, and a strong sense of camaraderie—qualities belying their age. She started asking questions about what he did, and after some time Yury began to answer them.

Nadia cast a discreet glance at Davin to make sure he was content with the silence. Just to be sure, she placed her hand on his thigh.

"He calls us Watchers," Yury had said of Karl during Nadia's brief recruitment period. "Our job is to protect the company's interests." Nadia met Braun once, at a café just over the French border, minutes from Geneva. He laid out the terms of their association and they agreed on her compensation package.

Her training followed. It was brief—only three months—but very intense. CORE had secured the services of a retired mid-level agent from the Swiss Federal Intelligence Service. Over the three months, she taught Nadia and three other Watchers the basics of tradecraft. After her "graduation," Nadia went on to accompany some of CORE's negotiators to third world countries. All her associates, and especially her employers back in Geneva, were quickly impressed with her results. She could get into any official or government agent's head—and heart—within days. She had the words, the posture, the perfect expression for every scenario. She was a natural.

Under the guise of a false identity and livelihood in Cyprus, and now through her fictitious assignment in Vienna, Nadia and the rest of the professional cleanup crew would protect CORE's interests by ensuring that Professor

Davin Valois of the University of Cambridge never returned to Cyprus.

Valois had found the coveted mineral through his government-sanctioned digs. He had opened the door for CORE to negotiate an exclusive lithium mining deal with Cyprus. All his steps had been monitored, and many had even been orchestrated, by his Watchers. They would methodically move in, use Davin's samples to ensure the deal was profitable, then turn things over to CORE's negotiators to secure the contract. Valois and his team would return to Cambridge and everyone would carry on happily.

The Vienna operation was not in the original plans. It had become a necessity after Davin had stuck his nose where he shouldn't have and become suspicious of the wires he'd found on one of Amiantos's slopes. It was an unexpected turn of events, but it was one that CORE was equipped to handle.

Farrouk's plan for Vienna was simple. Nadia would check into the Hilton with Davin. She would wine and dine him for two days, in a manner similar to their time in Cyprus. Then, on the eve of the fictitious fashion show, she would arrange for dinner at Café Central. She would go through all the motions of a romantic night out with her lover, and afterward, on the way back to the hotel, she would need to make a quick stop at a convenience store. She'd let him wait in the car, taking the keys with her.

Enter Farrouk's Watchers. One would storm the car from the back to take control of Davin at gunpoint. The other would meet Nadia inside and get the key. The two men would then drive Davin to Farrouk's location, a basement in the southern Viennese suburb of Liesing. There, Farrouk would interrogate the Frenchman to find out who knew about the wires Davin discovered at the lithium site. If necessary, they would use Farrouk's particular set of skills to extract the information they needed. Then they would kill him and get rid of the body in the woods nearby.

* * *

The following weekend: Vienna

At six o'clock on Friday afternoon, Davin was sitting at the ornate Café Central on Herrengasse, enjoying an "Amadeus"—a house favorite of double espresso with Mozart liqueur and whipped cream. He was reading an article about the recent lecture a Dutch scholar had given regarding the ice-melting effects of global warming. Though he seemed focused on the small screen in his hand, Davin was very much distracted by his excitement and anticipation.

He and Myra had arrived in Vienna the night before after a direct flight from Larnaca. Myra's fashion-show hosts (played to convincing effect by other Watchers) had arranged for a silver Mercedes to be parked at the airport's short-term parking. They'd driven the car, Myra at the wheel, to the Hilton Vienna, where, after settling into the room, they'd ordered room service. They showered, ate, and fell asleep in each other's arms by midnight.

Myra left early the next morning. "Last-minute details to firm up," she had told Davin as she pulled on her overcoat and pecked him on the cheek. Davin planned to sleep in a bit longer, then head out for some sightseeing. They had agreed to meet at Café Central for dinner.

Davin was trying to stay focused on the article at hand, but his eyes kept darting out the window, scanning for Myra. She would be arriving any minute.

Then his phone buzzed in his hand. Startled, he looked down and saw a text notification at the top of the screen. He tapped on it. The sender's identity was a long number sequence preceded by an asterisk and a couple of letters. The message read:

You were right about the wires. Myra is not who you think she is. You are in the middle of a trap, and your life is in danger. Leave Vienna ASAP!

His heart started pounding and cold sweat began to glaze his forearms and temple. Davin tapped a quick reply.

Who is this?

A red exclamation mark appeared next to his text, signaling that his message could not be delivered. He tried to resend it. Same result. Again. And again.

A hand tapped him on the shoulder. He jerked his head upward, his adrenaline levels soaring.

"What are you drinking? Looks delicious!" Myra said.

"Myra! You startled me. Uh, yes, of course. It's an Amadeus."

Nadia did not look down at his phone, and she never asked what he had been doing at the moment she joined him at the table. She had seen enough agitation on his face to know something was going on.

She effortlessly slipped into playing Myra, the exciting girlfriend on a business-and-pleasure trip with her French lover. She asked him about his sightseeing, and then over dinner she shared fabricated stories about the upcoming show. Davin, though still in shock from the mysterious text, kept his cool and carried on without any discussion of the incident.

Nadia waited for her chance all night. She found it when Davin slipped into the restroom shortly after a rather strained round of sex. Immediately after the bathroom door shut, she darted toward the nightstand on his side of the bed and turned on his phone. Within moments she found what she was looking for. The toilet flushed. Nadia reached for her own phone on the other side, turned on her camera, and began to snap some pictures of Davin's screen. The sink faucet was on. Nadia scanned the rest of his texts to make sure she hadn't missed anything, then froze as she heard the door handle turning. With the faucet still running, Davin cracked the door and poked his head out. Nadia barely had enough time to put down the phone and lie back on his pillow, putting on a most disingenuous smile. It was the first time in their entire relationship that, for at least a moment, she had lost control.

"Come back here," she said, "I miss you already."

Davin stayed calm, but all his senses were on high alert. "I actually have a better idea. Want to hop in the shower with me?"

They showered and watched some TV together. Then they took turns feigning sleepiness. Within minutes, the room was dark and completely still. Davin and Nadia faced opposite sides, their eyes wide open. Neither of them would get any sleep that night.

After about half an hour, Davin felt her stir and slip out of bed. He turned over and, faking grogginess, said, "What's up?"

"I can't sleep. Too much coffee today, I think. I'll go down to the gym for a bit."

Nadia changed quickly into gym shorts and a tank top. She draped a sweatshirt over her shoulders and placed her phone and headphones in the pocket.

"Be back soon," she blurted toward the door as she pulled it open.

In two seconds the door closed hard behind her, and then she was gone. It was the last time Davin saw her that night. They would only come into contact one more time.

Works for me, Davin thought as he pushed back the sheets and sat up along the side of the bed. He switched on his phone and swiped his thumb across the unlock prompt on the bottom. The screen still showed the text exchange Nadia had dug up while he was in the bathroom. With a look of anger and resolve, and through a series of jerky motions that expressed his feelings, Davin changed into some workout clothes of his own. He snatched the hotel key from the counter and left the room in a hurry. He made straight for the elevators, which he rode down. He was determined to confront Myra about checking his phone. He would tell her about the text he had received at the café, and then he would ask her point-blank what that was about. *It's crazy. We should be able to make sense of it*, he thought as the elevator doors swung open on the third floor.

When he got to the gym, the room was dark and the door was locked. He swiped his key at the card reader to get in. The lights came on as he stepped through the threshold. The place was empty and every machine was turned off.

Nadia's cab was moving south along Route 1, toward the *Stadtpark*. She was on her phone, speaking Russian. She had just texted two images from her phone to the caller on the other end. There was a pause on the line while the text went through. She turned around and nervously looked through the back window of the cab.

Viktor's voice on her phone broke the silence. He spoke slowly and calmly. "Americans, I'm sure of it. Moscow traced the number to Uzbekistan. The CIA routes messages through there all the time."

"I have to go. I have to contact the others."

"Do it."

Nadia called Farrouk and brought him up to speed on everything that had taken place that evening.

"We have to modify our plan," she said.

"Don't worry. We have it covered. The grey Volvo is at the place you know. I'll have a driver there for you shortly. Wait until I have confirmation about the Frenchman's movements. If he does what we expect, you'll follow him to the airport in the morning. The driver will get you there and help you with anything else you need. Book a flight to Geneva for both of you after it's done. You'll receive instructions from there."

"I left in a hurry. I have nothing. I'll need money for this cab fare, my passport, clothes for tomorrow."

"Go to the *Volkstheater* and ask your driver to wait. A man by the name of Khalid Homsi will arrive in a little while. He'll pay the fare and give you a bag. Everything you need will be in there, including your blond wig with the black roots. Take another cab to the Volvo."

"Nationality?"

"You know—'Myra.' Let me know when it's done."

Davin returned to the room and tried calling Myra. Six attempts all went straight to voicemail. His instincts told him to get ready, check out of the room, and run. But Davin couldn't help hoping that everything had been a big misunderstanding and they would sort through it all by morning. If things were worse than he hoped, and Myra didn't return by dawn, he would take the Mercedes and head to the airport.

Davin sat in an armchair by the window and looked down at the city below. Thoughts raced through his mind, intensifying the hollow feeling in his gut. After a while his weariness and frustration got the best of him. He fired up his laptop and typed out an email to Doug.

Things got very strange here in Vienna, Doug. I received a strange text from an unknown sender.

Davin explained the turn of events.

Unless Myra and I can meet and sort this out tonight, I'll catch the first flight to Larnaca in the morning. Please meet me at the airport.

Then he got up and began to pack.

The next morning, Davin followed the airport's signs to long-term parking. He veered right, made a couple mild turns, then eased the silver Mercedes to the entrance. His window already down, he reached toward the lit-up blue button. A ticket emerged at the bottom of the machine and the gate lifted. He proceeded into the car park.

A gray Volvo with tinted windows entered the car park seconds later. It had been following Davin for a few kilometers before he entered the airport loop, the last of a group of three cars that had left the Hilton hotel within five minutes of each other. A VW convertible was first, exiting the Hilton's car park seconds after Davin turned onto the *Vordere Zollamtsstraße*. Viktor, who drove the VW, followed Davin until just after he entered the *Franzensbrücke* bridge to *Weißgerber Lände*. Kristal, behind the wheel in a cream-colored Honda, passed her fellow Watcher at the bridge, taking over to trail Davin.

The gray Volvo, the last car in the Watchers' surveillance group, was already moving at 80 kph on the A4 motorway, the *Ostautobahn*, when Davin and the Honda entered the last 13-kilometer stretch to the airport. After Davin and Kristal passed the Volvo near the OMV, the massive Austrian refinery, the Volvo's driver kept up with Davin's Mercedes until he entered the airport's parker, while Kristal took the next exit off the highway. Khalid was driving the Volvo; Nadia was riding shotgun.

After finding full lots on the first and second level, Davin continued his search on the south side of the car park. He did not seem to be alarmed by the gray Volvo that was following him three or four car lengths behind.

Davin's brake lights and left turn signal registered faintly on the faces of the couple in the Volvo. He pulled into a parking space and turned off the engine. Grabbing his coat from the passenger seat, he opened the driver's side door.

The sound of a suppressed gunshot thudded softly in the air, followed by the pinging of a shell casing against the concrete.

Nadia emerged from the Volvo, which idled just ahead of the parked Mercedes. She picked up the casing with a gloved hand. After a quick look to ensure privacy was absolute, she approached the Mercedes.

Careful not to brush against the trickle of blood oozing from her victim's temple, she shoved the limp left leg back into the car and gently pushed the body sideways toward the passenger seat. She popped the trunk from the dashboard and shut the driver's door. With Davin's luggage in tow, Nadia jogged the short distance to the Volvo and got in. Khalid drove slowly and carefully up two levels and parked the car near the elevators. He placed the parking ticket under his floor mat and popped the trunk. While he was pulling his tan jacket and briefcase from the back, Nadia was disassembling her weapon. They would dispose of it by scattering the parts in garbage containers and street drains. She then pulled down the visor and applied a fresh coat of lipstick on her already-bright red lips.

She emerged from the car with her newly acquired bag and a faint smile for her accomplice, who was waiting by the rear of the vehicle.

They entered the elevator and pressed the button for Level 1: Departures.

Once in her seat on the plane, Nadia pulled out her phone and wrote a text. She held up the phone to show Khalid. He looked at it and nodded. She pressed send, and off the message went to Viktor. Just as the plane was taxiing for takeoff, Nadia sent one more text, this time to Dimitry Kanadov.

*   *   *

Limassol, Cyprus

"Dryovskaya has made contact. The Frenchman is dead." Dimitry walked over to the minibar, pulled out a bottle of Scotch, and poured two glasses. He handed one to Vasily.

"Her people must be happy with that."

"I'm sure they are, as our people will be as well."

"Well, good for her. Nadia has managed to please all her people at once." Vasily chuckled and lifted his glass. Dimitry laughed too and followed suit for a toast.

11
SLIPPERY SLOPE

June: Agios Mamas, Cyprus

Farrouk lives in Vienna.
Farrouk lives in Vienna.
FARROUK LIVES IN VIENNA!

Monir's eyes opened wide. He pushed back the covers and sat up in his bed, startled.

It had begun as a barely audible whisper deep in the recesses of Monir's subconscious. Every time the statement was repeated it moved him further from the realm of REM sleep and the jumbled-up dream fragments that generally characterized his last few minutes of rest. The volume increased until it reached the loud crescendo that jolted him awake.

It was his first thought of the day, a warning signal that bubbled up from inside of him.

"Farrouk lives in Vienna," Monir repeated to the sheets he had just pushed away from his torso and over his knees.

Monir retraced the thought pattern he had followed moments before he had drifted to sleep:

He had considered talking some more about Davin Valois with Stalo. The fact that she had spoken to him could be a promising start. He had planned to ask the residents of the nearby villages if they had seen any of Davin's team members. Next, strangely enough, he had contemplated calling Karl Braun. Karl always had his ear to the ground— he may have heard something.

But then Farrouk, a recent transplant to Vienna, due to his collaboration with CORE, had popped up in his mind. And somehow, between when he'd first thought of asking the man about the matter and that very moment, something inside Monir had highlighted Karl's Jordanian colleague and confidant not as a possible source of information but as a potential threat.

Over his many years in the field, Monir's discernment had enabled him to avoid negotiation landmines. Now his instincts were sounding alarms inside him. There was no way he'd be talking about this to Farrouk, or to Karl for that matter, until he had figured some things out for himself.

Monir was not closely acquainted with Farrouk. They had only met in person twice, and on both occasions Karl had done most of the talking. On several missions for contract acquisitions, Monir was aware that Farrouk's background

146

work had cleared the way for him by the time he arrived to do the talking. He never asked questions about Farrouk's finagling, as he was certain that the Jordanian's actions were shady at the very least. Monir's philosophy, which was also the primary reason for his longevity with CORE, was simple: Listen carefully, ask discreetly, and speak minimally.

Monir also knew that Farrouk employed a small team of disreputable characters to do his dirty work. Once, he had connected with some of them at Yangon's overcrowded business class lounge after signing a ruby-mining deal with the Burmese government. Though cordial, it was obvious from the Watchers' attitude that they didn't like him. He didn't much care for them either, but they had always managed to coexist peacefully, so long as the job got done.

If Davin Valois's murder had anything to do with the lithium deal in Cyprus—and Monir was almost convinced it did—Farrouk's goons were bound to be on the island. As long as he stayed true to his assignment, Monir thought, the Watchers would have no reason to be trailing him, which gave him a chance to keep an eye out for them. If he spotted any of them on the island, that would mean Farrouk was undoubtedly involved, and CORE foul play would be confirmed. Monir would have to watch his back.

But first things first, Monir thought. He had to prepare for his meeting with Angelos Mavros. It was scheduled for that evening at a coffee bar in the heart of Limassol.

Monir met Stalo the next morning at the spacious car park in the center of Pera Pedi. He pulled up next to her VW and parked his car. She would handle the driving from there. He had called the night before to ask if they could meet and talk. She agreed and suggested a drive along some of the most beautiful parts of the mountain region.

Stalo exited the car park and turned right on the main road to Mandria. Another right, seven kilometers up the road, and then right again by a sign that read "Agios Nicolaos 15 km." Numerous sharp turns followed, then a steep downhill descent through the easternmost portion of the Paphos Forest. About five kilometers into the forest, Stalo turned left onto a dirt road. It led to a river that wound its way into the Arminou Dam. Just ahead of Stalo's vehicle stood one of the region's most famous bridges. Stalo pointed at the bridge as she was turning off the ignition. "What do you think?"

"Nice, very nice," Monir managed. "But, please, finish what you were saying."

They'd been having a rather intense conversation almost from the outset of their drive in Pera Pedi. First, Monir told his story of the text message he had seen in Vienna back in January, shortly before his flight had departed for Geneva. Then he divulged all the information he had gathered two nights ago about the Davin Valois murder.

Stalo gasped, her hand over her mouth. "But…it couldn't be. Davin!" she cried.

Monir paused to let the news sink in. Then he spoke in greater detail about the economic implications of the lithium find. He mentioned nothing about CORE or Karl Braun, nor did he share his new suspicions about Farrouk.

"It's a huge deal, Stalo. We're talking billions. It could change everything around here." His eyes fixed on the distant horizon, Monir moved his hand back and forth directly above the dashboard, ending the motion with his finger pointing to their right. "All this could be carved up with roads, mining towns, and a massive industrial apparatus."

Beyond the edge of the two-lane road and the hundred-meter drop that followed spread a vast valley replete with vineyards and orchards and the small village communities they surrounded. Just above the iconic tiled roofs and the white church bell towers emerged the sheer rock faces of the westernmost peaks of the Troodos Range.

"If there's as much lithium in those mountains as we believe there is, it won't take long before they're erased from this gorgeous landscape." Monir paused, choosing his words carefully. "I believe things happen for a reason, Stalo. It was not coincidental that I intercepted that text on the plane, then was assigned the lithium deal on the very island where the Frenchman had been digging. Right by your village, too!"

Stalo nodded in agreement and motioned for him to continue.

"Generally, my company sends me in only after they've obtained sufficient evidence that they can make a fortune through the agreement I'll work to facilitate. My being assigned to the lithium deal means that a group initially unearthed the mineral, and then either the same team or another expedition followed up with more exploration and discovery."

Stalo nodded again, thinking. "I talked to Davin while he was still alive, you know," she told Monir. She described their brief interactions from the previous months. "It was always small talk about nothing of consequence. Like how everyone was doing, or how hot it was, or how much rain we had been getting—oh my God, Monir, the rain!"

"What about it?"

Stalo held up a hand to silence Monir, her other hand resting against her forehead. After a few seconds of thought she continued, speaking more slowly than before. It was evident that she was thinking about the events from months ago.

It had rained for days, Stalo recounted. One evening just after the rain had subsided, she had seen Davin and another man at the little grocery store in the village. They spoke of the rain and how terrible it was to be cooped up for so many days. "But then Davin's colleague said something about the rain also being 'a blessing in disguise,' as it pertained to their work, I assumed."

Monir was listening so intently that he wasn't paying any attention to the beautiful scenery unfolding before them in the Paphos Forest. "Did you ever learn more about what the man was referring to?"

"Not really, but it was evident something big was going on at the quarry, because on several occasions my dad came home from his fields saying government officials had been up there with their Range Rovers." Stalo looked into Monir's face for a reaction.

"Can we talk to your dad about this?"

"Of course. But at this time of day he's probably still out in the fields." Stalo looked around. "Can we stop here? Since we have some time, there's a hill nearby with a wonderful view that I want to show you. Your investigation can wait for at least a few minutes, right?"

She pulled over and Monir followed Stalo out the car. He did his best to indulge her and enjoy the scenery, but he was preoccupied with the latest developments. Stalo was aware of it but didn't push the issue. She was intrigued by the matter herself. They were on their way back to Pera Pedi shortly.

Monir's phone buzzed just as Stalo pulled up to his parked car. It was Angelos Mavros.

"Again, Mr. Young, my apologies for postponing last night's meeting. The president had just returned to Cyprus from a state visit, and I had to meet with his chief of staff. Well, it's all for our benefit anyway. But I'm sorry about the last-minute change of plans."

Mavros's call to postpone the meeting in Limassol had come while Monir was on his way to that very appointment. Mavros's explanation had been short and vague, and in light of Monir's growing concerns about CORE's actions, it was very unsettling.

"It's good to hear from you, Mr. Mavros. No problem at all. I look forward to meeting you whenever you can."

"Can you come to Limassol tonight?"

"Tonight?" Monir looked at Stalo. His mind was racing. Maybe they still had a chance to quickly talk to her dad before he headed back down the mountain to the city. The more information he had, the better. Perhaps the postponement of the meeting was fortuitous for him after all. Stalo nodded. She seemed to be tracking with him.

"Same place?"

"Yes. I'll see you there at nine o'clock. Mr. Theodorou will be joining us. He's the banker Mr. Braun—"

"I know him, Mr. Mavros. Nine o'clock it is."

Stalo and Monir arrived at the village around 4:00 PM. Her parents were sitting out on the shaded part of their patio, drinking coffee. A bowl of nuts sat between their two coffee cups.

Stalo got to the point. The geologists back in September. The heavy rains. Government vehicles showing up at the quarry. Did her dad remember those things? Was there anything else he could recall from that time?

Vangelis looked at his wife, then back at Stalo. He let out a sigh and reached for some peanuts, shooting a quick sideways glance at Monir. He spoke very slowly. Stalo translated after each sentence.

"I know the land, and the land knows me, especially in these parts. I've worked this soil my whole life. I know when things aren't right. I'm certain of it today, I have been for a while. There's trouble here." He looked at Monir, then back at Stalo. "Big trouble!"

Though calm and soft-spoken, Vangelis had conviction in his voice. This was not the first time he'd given thought to the matter. And that he had not said a word about it until he was asked increased his credibility with both Monir and Stalo.

His daughter prompted him to elaborate. Vangelis didn't know what they'd found at the quarry, exactly. But he knew it was big because of the government vehicles and the men who rode in them to the site. "I know about those officials. They don't leave their comfortable offices in Nicosia to look at rocks for days on end. They dug up something important up there. And then the drill. They brought a massive machine and worked it all day long. A couple of weeks later, they moved the operation up north to Farmakas, Kyperounta, Prodromos, and even all the way to Kykkos, I heard."

Vangelis looked beyond his porch toward the neighbor's fields across the street. There was more on his mind. He looked back at his wife, reading her face to know if he should say it. She nodded.

"It wasn't just them—the geologists and the government people. It's the others who came after them that worry me."

"The others?" Stalo was looking back and forth between her parents and Monir, who now leaned in closer to Vangelis.

"Foreigners started popping up in the area. You know how we live around here, Stalo, we have eyes and ears everywhere." He chuckled.

"The locals always pride themselves on knowing stuff," Stalo explained to Monir after translating.

"An American couple rented a condo on the outskirts of the village. The grocer's wife said her cousin saw them snooping around by the geologists' bungalows one night."

"Anyone else?" Monir asked eagerly.

Vangelis shot another glance at him warily, as though Monir had some responsibility in the matter. "A group of three—two men and one woman. They drove by the coffee shop in the center of town in a red Range Rover, way too many times for it to be a coincidence. They were looking for something, or someone. Then on my way from the fields one day, I saw them myself at the quarry. They were out of their car, walking toward the slopes beyond the roadblock the government had set up."

Monir nodded with appreciation. He was fully aware of the old man's apprehension. All he could do was try to gain his trust by the way he carried himself moving forward.

"What did they look like? What nationality were they, could you tell? Are you able to describe them, Vangelis?"

Stalo listened to her father and translated the descriptions for Monir. As one of the men in the village had stated, at least two of them were Russian. One man and the woman had stopped to buy some things from the coffee shop once. They spoke Russian. The other man had blond hair— European for sure, Vangelis guessed, maybe German or Scandinavian.

"Stalo, please ask him about the geologists. Anything he can tell us. Did they tell anyone about their work? When did they leave the village and why? Also, when was the last time he saw Davin?"

The old man shook his head. He didn't remember exactly, but the Frenchman was definitely gone by early February, which was when the team had packed up and left the cabins.

"Manolis—you know him, Stalo, the old man who sits at the coffee shop with his neighbors most of the day. He said the Frenchman wasn't with them when they loaded their cars."

Stalo smiled. She knew Manolis and his type. She despised busybodies, but in this case they were proving to be helpful.

Monir looked at his watch, then at Stalo. "Please express my thanks to your parents. Your dad has been most helpful.

Assure him that we will get to the bottom of this, and we will make it right."

Stalo conveyed only Monir's gratitude, leaving out the part about righting wrongs. She was skeptical about that promise herself.

"I have to get going to be ready for the meeting." He got up and extended his hand toward Vangelis. The man remained seated. He leaned his head sideways to look at his daughter, who was blocked by Monir.

"One more thing," Stalo translated. "The priest said one of the geologists went to church a few times. Said he had an Orthodox background. Maybe you can talk to Father Mattheos about it."

Within a couple of hours, Monir was driving to the city to meet Angelos Mavros and Giannis Theodorou. His mind was sifting through everything he had learned that day, especially the input from Stalo's father. The last comment about the churchgoing geologist was a new lead, one that Monir had already made arrangements to investigate.

The Saturday evening sun was behind Monir, making its last appearance for the day beyond the distant mountains in the west. Traffic was picking up in both directions on the road. In Monir's lane were the folks heading out for a night on the town. Those traveling north would be spending the weekend on their own or at their friends' and families' vacation homes in the mountains. Within just a few hours, the island's inhabitants—locals and tourists alike—would be shifting into Sunday mode, a weekly occurrence generally replete with relaxation, family visits, and food—lots of it.

Men in the villages would be lighting their backyard brick ovens before dawn to prepare their famous lamb *kleftiko*. Women would be mopping their porches and hosing down their sidewalks. Between 7:30 and noon, church bells would be ringing, summoning the faithful all across the island's cities and villages. And Monir, though by no means a churchgoer or someone interested in religion (as he confessed to Stalo), would find himself sitting in a pew at Stalo's church in Amiantos.

12

TRADECRAFT

January: Larnaca, Cyprus

The shot that killed Davin Valois came from Nadia Dryovskaya's suppressed .45 handgun. The sound the weapon made while firing the lethal bullet was minimal, due to both its custom-fit Osprey 45 silencer and the thick concrete walls of the airport's car park. Though no bystanders came forth to testify that they had heard the shot, its effects were heard around the world.

Langley, Virginia, heard it because Davin's last email to his friend Doug—which the Agency immediately intercepted through the Blakes—included his request that he be picked up at the Larnaca airport the next day. Doug had shown up to meet his friend, but an hour after the Vienna flight's last passenger had exited the customs area, Doug left the airport, bewildered that Davin hadn't informed him he'd missed his flight. Doug, of course, had no idea why Davin had missed the flight, and neither did he know that he had been watched by a wig-wearing Cynthia Blake. Five minutes after Doug gave up on waiting and rode the escalators to the airport's first level, Cynthia rose from her seat at the café in the arrivals hall—the spot she had occupied since half an hour before the plane's scheduled arrival—and sent a text to her husband and John Harden:

Valois did not arrive on the flight. Heading back to the condo. Recommending eyes on his friend, who just left the airport.

She also sent the five pictures she had snapped of Doug from her perch at the café while acting like she was fidgeting with her phone.

*   *   *

Limassol, Cyprus

The Russians did not have anyone at the airport that day. None of Moscow's agents had electronic surveillance on Davin or anyone else involved with the lithium deal. Nonetheless, the SVR knew about the Vienna killing almost immediately, thanks to the dependably loyal Nadia Dryovskaya.

Nadia took orders from Karl Braun as part of CORE's team of Watchers, but she worked for Russia first and foremost. The three-month tradecraft instruction she had received back when she signed on with CORE paled in comparison with the intense indoctrination and hands-on training by instructors—all of whom were former KGB agents—within the SVR's Directorate S. The ultra-secret initiative was responsible for planting Russian agents in foreign countries for surveillance, terrorist operations, and sabotage while remaining under deep cover, and Nadia fit the part perfectly.

Her mission from the very beginning had been to gain a foothold into Europe through her job at CORE and report back to Moscow on a regular basis. Other Russian operatives had reported a connection between CORE's CEO and prominent wealthy Arabs. When Farrouk entered the picture, Nadia received instructions to closely monitor the relationship between her boss and the new Jordanian recruit. In the meantime, SVR agents established the connection between Farrouk and ISIS.

Things accelerated once it became clear that the lithium deal in Cyprus was, from ISIS's point of view, another step toward hegemony in the region—an aspiration that was in direct conflict with Russia's plans. Nadia was told to stay on track with all CORE initiatives but be prepared to sabotage the lithium deal for her employers when the time was right.

Serving as a double agent was no problem for Nadia. She was paid well by both sides and enjoyed the thrill of tactical double-dipping. Of course, once she openly betrayed CORE she would have to disappear for a while.

"I see it as well-earned vacation time," she had told her Moscow handler.

*　　*　　*

Geneva

Karl Braun and the small group of CORE leaders were informed of Davin's shooting by Viktor. He'd emailed Braun, who then passed on the message to his associates:

The Italian prevailed over the French. Coast is clear.

None of the news came as a surprise to Braun. He had been intricately involved with the operation from the beginning, including the establishment of reliable surveillance on Davin, the selection of CORE's people in Cyprus and Vienna, Nadia's entrance and exit strategies, and even the backup plan in case Valois digressed from predictable behavior.

What Braun had not accounted for was the text Davin had received while sitting at Café Central in Vienna. The SMS created much concern and uncertainty for the German CEO because it invaded his otherwise perfect equation, an arbitrary and uncontrolled variable.

Braun ordered Nadia back to Geneva while they figured out who was behind the text. Viktor and Braun agreed it was likely the Americans. Viktor had been recruited by CORE after dropping out of specialized Russian intelligence training in the early 2000s. Though he never made it as a Russian operative, he'd had enough experience to be able to make that call, and Karl trusted his judgment.

Braun assumed that if the Americans had tapped into Davin's phone, they had also tapped into his email and who knows what else. They surely knew about Nadia's disguise as Myra Kortelli, and they probably knew her employers were interested in the lithium deal. But did they know that CORE was behind it all? Braun wanted to believe his cover was impenetrable, but he kept the question on the table just to be safe. His own experience had taught him never to underestimate the Americans' reach.

Nadia and Khalid arrived back in Geneva. Khalid was a Syrian ISIS operative whom Farrouk had insisted on bringing along when he relocated to Vienna. He was a sort of bodyguard, always by the Jordanian's side whenever Farrouk was in public, but sometimes he also collaborated with CORE's Watchers on various fronts, though only under Farrouk's orders.

After debriefing the two CORE operatives in his office, Braun dismissed the Syrian and told Nadia she was going to Nyon to take it easy for a few weeks until the dust settled from the Vienna incident. While pacing back and forth in the area between his desk and a large window that looked out onto Geneva's majestic scenery, he told Nadia his reasoning behind sequestering her in Switzerland for a while. "The Austrians will run their investigation, which, if things went as you told us, will turn up nothing. I'm not concerned about them. It's the Americans, or whoever sent that message to the Frenchman, that we have to look out for. I already have people on the case. We should know soon."

*   *   *

Nyon, Switzerland

Nadia was happy to stay within the borders of Switzerland, avoiding all airports and train stations. She enjoyed the amenities of the safe house and the Mercedes the company had provided for her. She also paid a visit to the local bank, where she deposited most of the 100,000 Swiss francs she had received for her latest accomplishments. The sum had been wrapped in silk and placed in a brand-new red Louis Vuitton handbag.

"Consider it a bonus for a job well done," Karl had said when he noticed Nadia was more interested in the handbag than the cash.

Just before leaving CORE headquarters, Nadia was informed that upon her return to Cyprus, her mission would be to "find, interrogate, and indefinitely neutralize" Doug Thomson, the man Davin had most certainly confided in regarding the explosives at Amiantos. Throughout the meeting with Karl, Nadia had been quiet, though attentive and engaged. She spoke up just as she was getting up to leave. "Who are you sending to Cyprus for the lithium deal?"

"One of our top guys," Braun said, "Monir Young. He was actually on the same flight you took from Vienna, there for some R&R. Did you see him?"

Nadia was running her right hand over her new bag, enjoying the feeling of the crocodile skin against her fingers. "No, don't know what he looks like. Never had the privilege of working with him. Heard great things though. I'm looking forward to meeting Mr. Young." She lifted her eyes from the handbag and looked out the window toward the Alps. "As things turn out, I find myself in need of a new boyfriend."

*　　*　　*

Ankara, Turkey

The Turkish government heard about the Vienna killing through a Turkish–Cypriot asset buried deep within the administrative apparatus of the British eavesdropping radar station at Agios Nikolaos. The undercover agent had picked up chatter, from yet-to-be-identified sources on the island, that the Frenchman who was heading the lithium expedition on Troodos had been killed. Foul play was undoubtedly the case. The man notified the agent he had been working with from Ankara, who in turn passed the message up the chain of command.

Turkey, through its own spy network—which essentially entailed the country paying for intel from well-informed freelancers in the business—was already aware of a foreign intelligence presence on the island, as well as CORE's workings to secure the lithium rights. They had bumped into CORE before, during a three-way spat with the company and Russia over iron ore in the Caucuses.

The news of Valois's murder was conveyed to the president with great concern, as it was evident that Cyprus's suitors for the deal were ruthlessly determined to have their way. After a few days of deliberations, and one last round of talks by Turkish negotiators in Nicosia, the president decided to back off from the deal. With many other domestic issues at hand and a promising long-term plan for a Turkish takeover in the region, he couldn't be bothered with the lithium. "Let them have it," he told his state secretary, "it's all going to be ours one day anyway. We've owned it all before, and we'll reclaim it once again when our caliphate is soon restored in all its glory."

*　　*　　*

Amiantos, Cyprus

Karl Braun had already arranged a plan for Doug Thomson. The Cyprus Watchers would monitor his activities and make sure he stayed put on the island until Nadia returned. They would also hack into his communications to see if he had any information about Valois's mysterious text in Vienna.

Thomson was easy to follow because his activities centered primarily on the lithium digs. With a wife of 35 years back home, as the Watchers ascertained from his emails, the geologist didn't seem at all interested in nightlife. He generally spent his evenings at the bungalow in the village and his weekends taking long walks or sightseeing with colleagues. As far as Dietrich and Yury were concerned,

Thomson was light work. They welcomed the slower pace and waited for Nadia to come back.

Around mid-March, once everyone at CORE was certain things were in order regarding Vienna, Nadia packed her bags and flew back to Cyprus on a direct Swiss Air flight from Geneva. She arrived in the early evening and was picked up in Larnaca by Yury. Though he was Russian, and despite their romantic history, Yury was oblivious to Nadia's involvement with the SVR in Moscow. He drove Nadia back to her luxurious apartment in Limassol and helped her carry up her luggage while the Evoque idled below. The two CORE operatives arranged to meet in the morning, with Dietrich joining them to discuss their upcoming mission to abduct and interrogate Doug Thomson.

Unbeknownst to them and to every henchman in Russia, Switzerland, and Vienna, all the Watchers' scheming would be in vain. Thomson would not be found in Amiantos or anywhere on the Troodos Range in the days to come. If fact, he would never be seen again by Nadia or her accomplices.

As Nadia was being driven back from the airport on the A1 highway toward Limassol, a white Lexus RX luxury SUV was heading in the opposite direction. In the front was a driver and a blond female in her forties. In the back was a gray-haired man. Doug Thomson sat beside him.

The American geologist had been notified of his imminent evacuation from Cyprus just 24 hours earlier. While at dinner with his team, Doug had walked into the restroom to wash his hands. A man he didn't know handed him a folded piece of paper.

"What's this?" Doug asked, starting to unfold the note. By the time he looked back up, the man was gone.

In familiar handwriting, the note said:

Doug,

Davin was murdered in Vienna by the same people who are now out for you. We are getting you out of Cyprus immediately. I'll fill you in about everything when you arrive back home. You fly out tomorrow night. Emirates Flight 108, Larnaca to Washington Dulles, through Dubai. Don't tell anyone about this, and do not use your phone or computer ever again. Your driver at Dulles will hand you new hardware. Do everything exactly the way I'm telling you. I'm asking you to trust me, Doug. Your life depends on it.

—Jeff

P.S. I don't work for forestry.

Doug rushed out the restroom and ran toward the restaurant's entrance. He scanned the patrons sitting at the dozen or so occupied tables. No sign of the man who delivered the note. Doug ran to the car park only to see the green Pajero that had just pulled out, wheels squealing, turning south toward Limassol.

The American returned to his seat, bewildered. When his colleagues asked if everything was all right, he answered affirmatively. He didn't mention the note.

As instructed, Doug never used his phone or laptop again. And by nightfall the next day, after minimal verbal interaction with the people who picked him up in the white Lexus, Doug Thomson was on his way to Dubai.

While Doug had finished dinner with his team, Cynthia Blake sat alone a few tables away. She was wearing walking shoes, khaki shorts, and a light blue blouse. Her eyes were concealed behind dark designer shades. Her left hand held the fork she was using to pick at her salad; her right hand, a cell phone. She thumbed a quick message before putting down the device and finishing her meal.

He got it. Seemed coy when he returned to the table. Looks like we're all set. Call the others.

13

REVELATIONS

June: Limassol, Cyprus

The meeting before the meeting. Angelos Mavros and Giannis Theodorou sat in the small tavern they had chosen for their talk with Monir. Mavros held his phone in his lap and spoke into a Bluetooth device in his ear. Theodorou sat across from Angelos, listening to the half of the phone conversation he could hear. Mavros was speaking to Orestis Sophroniou, giving the mining department chief a brief update on the happenings of the last few days.

"Where's the president on everything?" Sophroniou asked, anxiety in his voice. "Did you talk to Eleftheriou?"

"I did," Mavros said. He ripped open a sugar packet and emptied the contents into his French press coffee. "Costas said the big man's consent shouldn't be a problem. He has to be discreet, which we all anticipated from the beginning."

"Sounds vague to me. And who has to be discreet, Costas or the president?"

Mavros spoke very slowly, as though he were addressing a child. "It means, sir, that the president seems open to our recommendations about the deal but will not commit to anything just yet, definitely not publicly. As for Costas, as chief of staff he has to cover all his bases as well as the president's. So discretion is an absolute must for both. And for us, too."

"Does he understand the stakes? Do you?" Sophroniou snapped, his voice rising.

Mavros sipped his coffee. "You mean, does the president know that his budget, his beloved health reform bill, and, more importantly, his very reelection bid hinge on this deal going our way? Yes, he does. And do I understand that after this is over, we will all have the means to retire from our pathetic jobs? Yes, I do. But what you need to understand is that you're stressed, you're losing your nerve, and if you aren't careful you could end up doing something that, shall we say, affects your health."

Sophroniou took the hint. He didn't fear Mavros, but the Davin Valois matter was very much on his mind. He changed the subject. "When is Braun's negotiator getting there?"

"He's on his way now. Relax. Giannis is here. He says hi."

The mention of Theodorou seemed to have a calming effect on the senior official, who shifted to a pleading tone.

"Yes, hi, Giannis. Please, Angelos, if you can...if it works out, will you ask about the Frenchman? I'm still not comfortable...."

Angelos looked out the screened window of the tavern. A car had just pulled up outside. Though he'd never met Monir Young, he figured it was their man. He nodded toward Giannis, who straightened up in his seat.

Angelos smiled at the approaching Monir and spoke into his phone. "Like I said, sir, relax." He stood up, placed the phone in his pocket, and extended his hand toward Monir.

Initially, Monir was cordial with his two Cypriot liaisons. He let them do most of the talking. Stalo's teary eyes at Colors when she talked about Cyprus's history of exploitation, as well as her father's insight earlier that afternoon, had stirred up many questions inside of him. He was aware that a great injustice was about to be done—again—against the island-nation.

When Mavros and Theodorou were finished laying out their half of the lithium agreement, Monir surprised everyone, especially himself, by shifting the conversation drastically.

"Before we go any further, I have a few questions," he said, speaking rapidly. "What are the Cypriot government's long-term plans concerning the impact of new lithium quarries? Have environmental considerations been taken into account? How will the mountain communities be affected? And have you considered how the deal will affect the nation geopolitically? What about the implications for Cypriot–Turkish relations, for instance?"

Mavros and Theodorou stared at him, stunned. Monir continued, feeling the words flow from everything he'd been thinking about since meeting Stalo.

"What are the contract stipulations regarding the pace of the excavation? Will there be compensation for the villagers that may be displaced? What is your government's position regarding miners—has a union been notified about representing them?"

Monir would have carried on had he not been interrupted by Theodorou, who raised his hand and leaned forward.

"Please, Mr. Young. We have the mineral, your company has the means to secure the rights for unearthing and possibly even marketing this lithium. Don't you think you should focus on your part and let us handle the local matters?" He leaned back and made eye contact with Mavros. "Isn't that what Mr. Braun would expect from us all?"

Monir's stomach twisted, but he stayed composed. He decided to poke further. "The geological team that found the mineral—where are they now? Are you still in contact with them?"

Mavros jumped in. "Their job was done after they completed the drilling and provided reports about their findings. All the people who constituted that team returned to their countries in March."

"Have you stayed in touch with their leadership? The Frenchman who headed up things in Cyprus and his boss at Cambridge? We may need to speak with them if questions arise during our negotiations."

"Yes, we are in close communication with them," answered Mavros. Giannis elaborated with a statement that sent chills down Monir's spine.

"We talked to Dr. Wiley and Valois just a few weeks ago, didn't we, Angelos?"

"Yes, we did, and they are standing behind their findings and projections."

The warning signal Monir had sensed when he was jolted out of sleep a few mornings back returned—and it was stronger. From that point on, everything was a blur to him.

They talked for another 15 minutes about the projected timeline on which everything would transpire, then the three men parted ways.

It'll be a rough ride back up to Agios Mamas, thought Monir, who felt sick to his stomach. For the first time in a long time, he was both disgusted and afraid. Not because he was shocked by the two Cypriot men's lies. Insincerity and dishonesty were always deal-making factors among CORE collaborators. Monir had come to anticipate half-truths and lies in every endeavor to exploit natural resources, and he certainly expected to encounter corruption. In fact, Monir's success for more than 20 years with CORE was in large part the product of his ability to leverage corruption to his advantage.

But through all the deals he'd handled in his time, Monir had never gotten as close to anyone as he had to Stalo. Of course he knew his negotiations had a very real effect on the lives and livelihoods of people in Ghana, Egypt, Chile. But before Stalo, he'd never bothered to care about the human side of what he did. Before Stalo, he'd never had to.

But now his discomfort with his job and his employer was mounting. Moreover, Mavros and Theodorou had an edge: the ear and longstanding loyalty of Karl Braun. Monir knew it wouldn't be long before Theodorou phoned Braun to tell him the content of their discussion at the table, including Monir's not-so-well-received questions.

His apprehension was magnified by the fact that if his suspicions were correct about Davin Valois's demise, it would be the first time he'd been confronted with the violent elimination of one of the key players in a deal, not to mention an obvious cover-up of the incident. The question was, was Braun behind it, or were the Cypriots? Either way, an evil scheme was at work, and by the way Theodorou had mentioned Braun, it sounded like the German CEO and his goons had crossed a line. Manipulating a corrupt system was one thing; cold-blooded murder was another.

More thoughts. More discomfort. Even if Braun wasn't directly involved in killing Valois, he was definitely aware, and consenting, of it. So any step away from Braun and CORE's prescribed course of action would be a step toward the point of no return for Monir.

As far as he was concerned, the deal was off, at least until the murder of Davin Valois was properly sorted. Monir would keep up appearances and go through the motions, but he'd also intensify his efforts to get to the truth.

The weight of the entire matter was bearing down on Monir from every side. As though to convey how rotten things had become, a stench hit Monir just as he was about to take the turn toward Alassa and the Kouris Dam. There they were, seven garbage trucks convoying slowly up the winding mountain roads. *Stalo was right,* he thought, *it stinks to be behind these trucks. Stalo's been right about everything.*

The next morning, Stalo picked up Monir outside his condo. He told her about his meeting with Mavros and Theodorou as they drove to Stalo's church. Stalo listened intently, with occasional grunts of disapproval for her countrymen. Monir laid out his thoughts about CORE and Braun's likely involvement in Davin's murder.

At the church, they parked near the courtyard entrance. A few other people were walking toward the church from the car park. Monir and Stalo lowered their voices as they approached the gate, hearing chanting inside. Whiffs of incense had found its way to their noses through the open windows on the side of the building.

"We will have to finish this talk later," Stalo said while scanning the interior for a seat. She led the way to an empty row about halfway down and to the right. Everyone was standing, which made Monir less self-conscious about his first church appearance in decades. With nods and smiles, Stalo greeted a few acquaintances. Monir kept his eyes on the back of her neck until they had reached their seats.

He looked around the room, taking in everything. Dozens of hand-painted icons in the front and on the side. Ornate woodcarvings all around, painted with gold. And a large display case with glass on the front and sides. It stood on the left near the front of the sanctuary. Stalo later told Monir that the case contained the bones of some of the saints, as well as some of their personal belongings.

As he took in his surroundings, Monir caught the stares of a few churchgoers. Their faces were solemn, their looks cold. They obviously disapproved of a daughter of Amiantos bringing a foreigner to church with her. *Nothing like being fuel for the fires of local gossip*, Monir thought.

A priest was chanting verses of Scripture from the large Bible that was spread on a table waist-high in front of him. Two psalmists, one on each side of the altar, frequently interjected with short chants, most of which ended with a word Monir understood well, "Alleluia."

In a few minutes the priest finished his chants and looked up. His light blue eyes matched the color of the sea along the Cypriot coastline. His face conveyed maturity but also youthfulness. His expression was calm and inviting. Tall and well built, his feet firmly planted by the center of the altar, he certainly did not fit the stereotype of the meek-and-mild clergyman that Monir had in his mind.

"Is that the priest your dad spoke about?"

His question jolted Stalo from a room-scan of her own.

"Yes, that's him, Father Mattheos."

"I like him."

"Me too. Everyone does."

The church service had long been dismissed. Monir and Stalo were seated in the thick shade of the vine beside the priest's house. After the liturgy ended, Stalo had approached Father Mattheos in the church courtyard. Would he be willing to meet with her and her friend regarding the quarry matter? He'd agreed and told them to come by that afternoon, on the condition that Stalo would handle the translation. "My English no good," he said, smiling at them.

His wife had just poured water in their glasses from a ceramic pitcher. Father Mattheos offered his guests fruit from the wide bowl of cherries, plums, and peaches in the center of the table. Monir opted for a plum. Stalo went for the cherries. The holy man started in on a succulent peach. His wife took a seat beside him and smiled at Stalo.

Monir looked up at the vine. "Looks like it's going to be a great year for grapes, Father."

Stalo translated.

"Indeed it does, Mr. Young. As long as we can keep the birds from them, we should have a good harvest in August and September."

Stalo thanked the couple again for having them and got to the point. The mineral the geologists found by the quarry—did Father Mattheos know about that? The priest nodded affirmatively. Stalo continued. Her father had talked about one of the geologists attending the church at some point. "Was he Orthodox?"

"Thomas. I don't know his last name. I never asked. Austrian with an Orthodox background—his mother's side was Greek, I think. He came to church almost every week. We spoke quite a bit, actually. Thomas told me there was a lot of government supervision surrounding their work. They dug up many, many places all over this range." The priest swept his hand across the empty space to illustrate.

"Did Thomas seem concerned at any point?" Stalo asked. "Was there ever mention, on his part, of specific issues about the way our government was handling things?"

The priest's wife began nodding before Stalo finished the question. Her husband looked at her, cuing her to continue.

"Mavros. I believe that was the name of the official Thomas didn't like," she said.

Monir jerked his head slightly to the right at the familiar name.

The woman continued. "He'd been assigned to accompany the team to the various drill sites. Thomas said Mavros was a character. He was shifty when he spoke, spent a lot of time on his mobile, and was disrespectful to the team, especially the women."

Stalo looked at Monir, who asked, "Did Thomas talk at all about the Frenchman who led the expedition? His name was Davin. Davin Valois."

"Not by that name," responded the priest, "but he did say something once about their leader. Said he had to do extra work that Sunday because the leader was in Venice with his girlfriend...or was it Vienna?"

"Vienna," confirmed his wife.

Monir felt his stomach churn. "When was that? Do you remember?"

"After Christmas and New Year's. Sometime in January, I'd say."

Monir looked at Stalo for a long moment after she'd finished translating. "Any idea where we can find more information about him or the woman you mentioned?" he asked the priest.

Father Mattheos did not have more to offer, but Stalo and Monir thanked him and his wife profusely for their help. There was a woman involved with Davin. Finding her could finally shed some light on his murder.

14
COUNTER-PLOTTING

June: Agios Mamas, Cyprus

Monir and Stalo operated mostly in the evenings after Stalo got home from work, roaming Amiantos and several surrounding villages to ask shopkeepers and coffee shop regulars about the Frenchman and his female companion. It was their third night on the prowl when the owner of Skia, a coffee shop in Farmakas, answered their query by pointing to two men playing backgammon in the back of the outdoor patio. Manolis and Stamatis, both in their late 60s, said they knew the Frenchman, as he had stopped there for coffee regularly during the time he worked out of the quarry. And they'd seen the woman with him a couple times.

"Russian," Manolis offered in his course voice. "Definitely Russian. Tall. Good-looking." He smiled at his friend. "Long blond hair."

Stamatis contributed an observation of his own. "She drove. Both times. A red Range Rover. Russians like those."

The red vehicle was exactly what they needed. Finding a car with that description was surely much easier than continuing to look for a tall, blonde woman. They thanked the men and turned to leave.

"You're not the first ones to come here looking for information, you know," Stamatis said.

They stopped. "What do you mean?" Monir asked.

"Two other Americans stopped by, not too long ago. Drove a green Pajero. We didn't talk to them, and we don't really know who did, but we heard they were asking similar questions." Stamatis looked at Manolis, seeking confirmation. It was clear that Manolis had more clout in the place.

"He's right," Manolis confirmed. "And then there was this white Lexus, twice it was here. A blonde woman got out and bought something at the counter. Asked if the owner had seen a woman driving a red Range Rover." Manolis looked hard at Stalo. "It's because of who you are that we're talking about this. We know your father, and we knew his father, too. You come from good stock. Be careful with these foreigners."

Stamatis interjected. "Every mess we've ever gotten ourselves into started with foreigners wanting the good of this land and being willing to do whatever it takes to get it."

"They found something big up there at that quarry," said Manolis. "And they're all swooping in like seagulls during a fish frenzy to gobble it up. Make sure you're on the right side of things. And watch your back."

Back at the car, Monir offered to drive. "What was that all about?"

"Nothing. Just Cypriot men being Cypriot men. They always formulate opinions based on information they've gathered by watching everyone who comes and goes, and by hearsay, and then they self-appoint themselves as gurus that can lecture the younger people."

"What were they lecturing you about?"

"About the potential danger in our pursuit. And, if I'm being really honest, Monir, deep down, I believe them."

Monir seemed a bit confused. "You do, huh? Didn't think you put much stock in coffee shop advice."

"Generally, I don't. But somehow there are times when those men are accurate, Monir. They may be rough and uneducated, and sure, many of their ideas are derived from the papers or from gossip, but they are also men who have lived through a lot, and their experiences contribute to a keen sense of discernment. They just know some things.

Most of the time I ignore them, but I also know when it's time to heed their advice."

Monir took a moment to ponder the thought as he rounded the sharp bend just outside the northern boundary of Amiantos. "So, they're saying we could be in deep waters. I agree. What's their advice?"

"It's not that clear with them. It's the tone, the timing, the intensity in their eyes…I don't know just what it is, but I know they're right." She paused to catch her breath. "Monir, I'm unsettled about this whole thing." Her voice broke. She looked out the window to remove her teary eyes from his line of sight.

Stalo's gaze remained on the distant hills beyond her village for a few moments. Then she felt Monir's fingers rest on her hand and curl downward for a gentle squeeze. It was the first time they had made physical contact. She turned her palm upward and firmly clasped Monir's hand. With the exception of the times he had to use his hand to shift gears, they remained that way for the remainder of their drive to his condo at Agios Mamas. Nothing more was spoken by either of them for a while.

When Monir pulled up outside, he shut off the engine and waited, his eyes fixed on a thicket of olive trees in the field just ahead. She moved her hand from his and wrapped it

186

around the spot just above his elbow. They turned toward each other simultaneously.

"I hope you know what you're getting us into, Monir."

"We're in it together, that's what I know. And it's all I need to know, for now."

They leaned forward and kissed. It was short, somewhat exploratory at first. They stopped and looked at each other. No one spoke. A second kiss followed, more passionate. Then another. They embraced tightly and continued to kiss. Her hands were moving quickly through his hair; his stayed around her ribcage, pulling her close.

They left the car and continued inside Monir's condo. Her fears seemed to be alleviated, and the weight of the case lifted from his shoulders. They were together, and at least for tonight, that's all they knew.

It was almost midnight when Monir's phone began to buzz. He'd been lying awake, thinking things through. Stalo had dozed off beside him. There had been a steady breeze blowing down from the mountains and entering the room through the open veranda doors.

The vibration of the phone against the nightstand jolted Stalo in her sleep. Monir put a hand on her shoulder, his other arm reaching for the phone. He left the bedroom and walked toward the kitchen.

"Hello, Karl. Working late, are you?"

"Monir."

"To what do I owe the honor?"

"Your indiscrete line of questioning, for one. Giannis Theodorou and his friend Mavros have been wondering why my negotiator doesn't seem to be on the same page as the rest of the team."

Monir's experience with Braun, and especially his instincts at that moment, warned him to opt for silence. He remained quiet and waited.

"Since when do you, Mr. Young, concern yourself with unions, demographics, and the environment when it comes to closing a deal? Or government policy? Or the ethics of it all? And what's it to you if the mountain villages get uprooted?" Karl paused conspicuously. "Getting too close to the locals, are you?"

Monir looked in the direction of the bedroom. *Karl couldn't possibly have*— He chose not to go down that road. Instead, he managed a calm response. "Just asking some questions, Karl. Maybe you're reading too much into things."

"Am I? There's a meeting with the president's chief of staff in two days. The only questions coming from you will be 'Where do we sign?' and 'Where do you want us to wire your money?'"

"I understand."

"Watch your step, Monir."

"I intend to."

"I hope so. And just so we are perfectly clear, no more poking around the villages for information about a French geologist and his girlfriend. Instead, focus on getting the job done, so you can hold on to *your* new girlfriend. It would be a shame if your little infatuation didn't last past tonight."

The line went dead.

Karl's call, particularly his parting advice, had validated all of Monir's fears. The CEO's final comment confirmed his involvement in Davin Valois's murder, and he had also implicated CORE by telling Monir to stay away from the subject.

Then came the torrent of questions about the most serious matter.

At what point did Karl's goons latch onto him and Stalo? How far back did CORE's surveillance go? And was it done by individuals watching them or through technology? Was the condo bugged with mics, cameras, both? Could they see him sitting by his kitchen table at that very moment?

He decided to assume the worst. Monir rushed to the bedroom, closed the doors to the veranda, and drew the curtains. Using the light from the kitchen window, he scribbled a note to Stalo, folded it in half, and left it on the kitchen table under her coffee mug.

We are not safe here any longer. Much to explain. House may be bugged. Act normal, but say nothing about "the case." We have to get ready quickly and then leave this place—for good.

Then Monir scribbled another note, this one to himself. It was a plan, a list of tasks that had to be undertaken in the next 48 hours:

1) *Look for the three cars (green Pajero, white Lexus, red Range Rover)*

Monir thought that even if Karl was closely monitoring them, there was no way he could have known about the information the two men had given them just hours earlier at the coffee shop. The men had clearly stated that the only reason they were forthright with information was because they were talking to Stalo, a woman from their village.

2) *Find out if there are honest government officials who can work with us to block the deal. Where does the president really stand?*

3) *Look for possible connection between Davin's girlfriend and CORE*

If the woman was one of Braun's Watchers, CORE would be directly implicated in Davin's murder. Shutting down CORE might be the fastest way to spare Cyprus, and the world, of a bad lithium deal. Monir was done operating in the defensive mode of investigation. He was going on the offensive. He would partner with Stalo and any local or foreign asset to uncover and fully expose his company's schemes. Why had he never recognized CORE's evil ways before? How could he have been so blind—even to help facilitate such wrongdoing over the years? What made the difference in this case?

He heard Stalo stirring in the bedroom. "Monir?"

A surge of fear shot into his gut at the thought of Karl's last comment. "Be right there."

He thought of two more items but did not add them to the list: *Keep Stalo out of CORE's crosshairs, and revisit Father Mattheos.*

Monir and Stalo left his condo an hour after sunrise. Assuming the house could be under video surveillance, Monir took only a handbag of clothes. He would make a few trips back over the next few days for the rest of his belongings, so as not to arouse suspicion.

Considering that his car may have been bugged as well, Monir stuck to small talk on the drive back to Stalo's home at Amiantos, mostly asking questions about Stalo's work. She played along well, acting perfectly normal.

Once they got to a safe place, Monir would fill Stalo in on everything that had transpired while she was sleeping. Then he would share his plan of attack and move forward with her by his side. He was still shaken by his talk with Karl, but now that the sun had come up and Stalo was talking with him, Monir felt more optimistic about things. In spite of the developments with Karl, Monir was riding high in the afterglow of the previous night. If he could only catch a few hours of sleep at Stalo's, he would certainly be able to make progress throughout the rest of the day.

But neither he nor Stalo had any idea how badly they'd been compromised, how closely they were being watched, or how deadly things were about to become.

*   *   *

April: Geneva

The mysterious text Nadia had intercepted back in January—the night before she killed Davin—had thrown Braun and Farrouk into a frenzy to try to track down who had sent it. Its timing and content reflected the work of professionals. The disappearance of Doug Thomson—made

192

known to CORE the day after Nadia had returned to Cyprus—was of even greater concern.

Someone was on to CORE and its Cyprus interests, most likely a foreign intelligence agency. But which one? CORE had many enemies and few friends in the world of espionage. Karl made it a habit to recruit ex-intelligence agents to fill his Watcher ranks, paying handsomely for the expertise and inside knowledge they brought from their former employers. The practice had not done much to endear CORE to the intelligence community, but Karl thought the benefits balanced out the increased attention it brought the company.

The British and the French would be out for vengeance, as Braun had repeatedly snatched gold and diamond mines under their noses in Africa. The Americans would want to expose CORE's money laundering in order to get ahold of large sums that were held in the States or in U.S.-owned banks worldwide. The Russians had a bitter taste after the Caucasus showdown. To Braun's knowledge, he had never crossed the Israelis, but then again he would not put it past them to collaborate with other agencies.

For how long had CORE been in the crosshairs of whoever was behind the text and Thomson's disappearance? What was their objective? And, more importantly, what were they plotting next? Braun and Farrouk had a few leads here and there, but nothing definitive, and certainly nothing against which the Watchers could launch a counteroffensive.

Then Karl had an idea. Nadia was already in Cyprus, and by her own admission, whether she was speaking facetiously or not, she was "in need of a new boyfriend." Being that Monir was driving the lithium deal for CORE, he would be of great interest to CORE's enemy. If he and Nadia got together, whoever had been watching Nadia while she was with Davin would probably latch onto Monir as well. All CORE would have to do is watch Monir and they would soon have their answers.

Farrouk liked the idea but had one question. "OK, we'll throw in Monir as bait and wait to see which fish comes for him. But why arrange for him and Nadia to get together?"

"Because we have to assume that Monir is unknown to these people. If they had wanted Nadia, they would have already made their move. She's not directly involved with the deal. He is."

"So use her as bait as well?"

"Right. On her own, she's not enough. Think of Nadia as the scent that would help direct the big fish to the bait."

Farrouk nodded. "You want me to set up full surveillance on Monir in Cyprus?"

"Exactly."

"I'll take care of it. Condo, car, the works."

Yury and Dietrich placed pinhead-sized cameras and listening devices in Monir's condo a few days before he arrived. Nadia placed a tracking device under the frame of his rental. She planned to insert a mic inside the car after she managed to get close to him.

What everyone had not factored in—a twist that proved to be problematic—was Monir's car falling in a ditch and his subsequent rescue by the old man, Vangelis. The incident led to Monir meeting Stalo, which messed things up for the Watchers on several counts: For one, Monir's car was out of commission, and until his new rental was sorted out, Stalo drove him everywhere. Her car was not under surveillance, as she, and the intensifying romantic interest between her and Monir, was completely unknown to the Watchers until later. When they finally found out, another complication became evident, as Monir's attraction to Stalo shut out Nadia from attempting to get close to him. Seduction would not work with Monir, and seduction had always been Nadia's strong suit.

Once the connection was established between Monir and Stalo, Yury and Dietrich kept an eye on Monir by following his or Stalo's car. Sometimes the Watchers switched rental cars; at other times they watched from a distance through high-powered camera lenses or binoculars. They also talked to the shopkeepers or coffee shop patrons with whom the couple had spoken.

The footage from Monir's condo, when he and Stalo spent the night together, gave Karl an additional edge. When Nadia messaged the German boss to inform him she was emailing an "amusing video from your rogue negotiator's bedroom," Karl was elated. He would call Monir that same night and indirectly invoke the footage to let Monir know that he and his girlfriend were being watched.

"That should keep him sedated until the deal is signed," Karl explained to Nadia, "or at least until you and your team arrange for a more effective and permanent solution."

She snickered. Karl finished the call with one last directive.

"Time to get one of Farrouk's little incendiary toys involved. Give him a call."

15

THE HELP

June: Nicosia, Cyprus

Costas Eleftheriou was on edge during his Friday briefing with the president. He always felt the most persuasive when he was free to pace the floor, making a case with hand gestures and body language. But shortly after Eleftheriou began to bring the president up to speed on Monday's meeting with CORE, Cyprus's chief executive pointed to an armchair and told his chief of staff to take a seat.

The president got up from his imposing brass-studded leather chair and walked around his desk toward Eleftheriou. He pulled up a chair from the other end of the room and sat in front of his 49-year-old aide. The leader spoke calmly but firmly, looking straight into Costas's eyes.

"I've always asked not to know details about a lot of the matters you handle for me. It's better for all of us that way. But the details I'm not aware of, in this particular case, worry me. Especially the background story of this Swiss company that showed up back in November, when we first started to explore our options for the mineral rights."

"I can explain, Mr. President—"

The president's hand went up swiftly. "Not now—I want you to listen to me! When we got news of the lithium, we knew that a venture of this magnitude would undoubtedly attract foreign interest. We had every expectation to hear from Russia, the U.S., the British, and, of course, the Turks up north. We prepared for state delegations, business entities, even representatives of intelligence agencies. But how does CORE, without any state support and without any history of doing business here, end up with a front seat in this negotiation process?"

Eleftheriou tried to echo the president's calm tone. "Well, they heard about the deal from contacts they've made in Cyprus over the years. And they seemed to be in a financial position to pursue it. So…"

The president had a slight smile on his face as he looked at Costas.

"Contacts, eh? From what sector of our economy are those contacts, Costas? Banking, perhaps? Ministry of the Interior? Mining?"

What on earth is happening? Costas wondered. Did the president's line of questioning signal a roadblock of what everyone had worked so hard to accomplish, or was the leader of Cyprus simply trying to get as good a handle on the deal as possible before committing? Costas cringed at the thought of how the others would perceive this turn of events.

The president stood up. "I'm coming to the meeting on Monday. I have a lot of questions for everyone. You, CORE, and all their *contacts* had better be prepared."

He walked around his desk and sat down. Putting on a pair of glasses that were lying on top of a book, he began to leaf through some documents.

"Mr. President, I don't think it's a good idea to—"

"We're finished here Costas. Have a good weekend. I'll see you on Monday."

*   *   *

Athens, Greece

Chandy set the phone down and adjusted his earpiece. It was ringing on the other end. Harden would be coming on at any moment. Chandy drew back the curtain and scanned the view. He was at his old standby hotel in Glyfada, on the southwestern tip of the Athenian peninsula. The deep blue Aegean waters below, cloudless skies above.

"Harden here."

"Hey, John, it's me."

"Oh, hey, man. Didn't recognize the number. You in position?"

"I'm using a different phone. Yes, I'm here. What've we got?"

"Give me your update first."

"Our info coming out of the mining department linked us to a banker in Limassol, who in turn seems to be connected to CORE."

"How closely connected?"

"Is $50 million close enough for you? Also, CORE sent in a man a few weeks ago. He doesn't strike us as a thug—more like a negotiator."

"Makes sense. Have you been watching him?"

"Cynthia was about to set up shop at his place but the bug sensors on her scanner went crazy even before she got to his door. Someone beat us to him."

"Who do you think? Russians?"

"We've been tracking a Russian woman, but we don't think she's representing Moscow. She works for CORE. You know her."

"Vienna Girl?"

"Yup, same woman. Goes by Myra Kortelli. Cynthia Blake's been on her since she got back from Geneva in

March. After we got Thomson out of Cyprus, Kortelli started her preparations for this new guy's arrival."

"Name?"

"Monir Young. Iranian American, according to the State Department."

"Iranian American? Interesting. But wait, why would CORE be keeping tabs on their own man? Is it company policy, or is something else going on?"

"This is where it gets interesting, John. While we were scratching our heads trying to figure out a way into this guy, Young sort of walked right to us. Somehow he got connected to a local girl from Amiantos, the village by the quarry. Tyson and Cynthia got wind of him because they're staying around there. They found out he's been poking around in the area ever since he arrived. He sure doesn't seem to be following CORE's script."

"You think he has his own agenda?"

"Maybe, but not by the questions he and the girl have been asking. They seem to have made the connection between Kortelli and Valois. And by all indications, they're also turned off by the Cypriot officials. The guy's turning into a boy scout against his own people, if you ask me."

Harden was silent for a few moments.

"Everything OK, John?"

Harden was looking out the window at the tops of the trees on the outskirts of the Langley campus. How he'd love to trade the woods of Virginia for the Athenian coastline just then. "Our orders from the beginning were to shut down CORE, period. If one of their own is working to that end, all the better, right?"

"Yeah, except we'd have to keep an eye on him, and that increases our chances of being spotted by the Russian and her two goons. Three, actually: Tyson said another one arrived just yesterday. We know him, too—Vienna Boy."

"Well, keep an eye on Young. And give him a hand if he needs it."

"We'll do what we can. Anything else?"

"Yeah, Moscow—what are their people up to over there?"

"Distant. Nowhere near the action. They don't seem too interested."

"Either that or they're being sly about it. Is it possible they have someone there we don't know about?"

"Maybe, but that person would have to be pretty good for us not to know about them."

"And the others?"

"Doing their thing. You know how they are. But we're in touch, and that's good."

"OK. Say hi to Eli for me. I like the old man."

Giannis Theodorou heard about the president's decision to attend Monday's meeting from Angelos Mavros, who Eleftheriou called minutes after exiting the president's office. Theodorou passed on the news to Braun in Geneva.

"Imbeciles! We're dealing with complete imbeciles!"

"What can I say, Karl? We were surprised as well. I guess none of us can control how the president thinks."

The comment infuriated Braun even more. He slammed his open palm against his desk.

"No! I will not accept your damn excuses!" he roared into the speaker phone. It was a rare flare-up of emotion. Karl could be cunning and ruthless, sometimes outright vicious, but showing anger this nakedly was out of character for him. He paused for a moment to regain his composure, then continued.

"Generally, heads of state *think* about things that can build or tear down their power base. You and your friends over there have been paid good money to ensure that your president perceives our arrangement only as an asset, and by no means as a threat to his administration. If he's asking hard questions and is now planning to attend this meeting, it's because someone didn't do his job."

"Karl, I can fix this—"

"You've done enough. I'll clean up this mess myself."

$*$ $*$ $*$

Monir had just left Stalo's house and was on his way to a hotel in Kato Platres. He had suggested that he base out of her home at Amiantos, at least until Monday's meeting was behind them, but she firmly declined. As liberated as she may have felt from village conservatism, Stalo wasn't anywhere close to having her new lover move in with her, even for a few nights.

"Not in a small village like Amiantos, where everyone sees and talks about everything," she'd said.

They'd agreed to meet at Stalo's church later to talk to Father Mattheos. Monir was deep in thought, planning what he wanted to say to the priest, when his phone started buzzing, startling him. He had been on edge since his conversation with Braun the night before. The few hours of sleep he'd gotten on Stalo's couch, with Stalo next to him, had certainly had a calming effect on his nerves, but now a knot reappeared in his stomach. He would never admit it to Stalo, and he really didn't want to come to terms with it himself, but deep down Monir knew that he was in over his head. He feared that neither his newfound romance nor his rudimentary plan would hold up against Karl Braun's formidable arsenal against him.

The caller ID was blocked, but moments after answering, Monir knew who was on the other end.

"Have you thought things over, Monir?" Braun asked in a fatherly tone.

The knot pulsated, sending a wave of fear through Monir's body. "I have. I'll do my job, Karl."

It was a slightly vague answer, but the German didn't pursue it.

"Good man. I've always known you to be reasonable. Listen, now that we have an understanding between us, I want to fill you in on some developments. I received word that the president wants to attend Monday's meeting as well."

"I see. That's certainly news to me." Monir's mind was spinning as he tried to guess what had precipitated that change.

"The man has some questions for us, which is not a problem—but just to make sure he gets the right answers, I'm coming to the meeting as well." Karl paused for a reaction from Monir. Hearing nothing, he continued. "I fly in on Monday morning. I'll email you the details. Arrange for a car to pick me up at the airport and take me straight to the capital from there. Book the Nicosia Hilton for one night. That's where the meeting is being held, yes?"

"Yes. That's right. I…I'll take care of it for you."

"Good man."

Monir was still in a daze when he arrived at the hotel. He could hardly recall anything from the 20-kilometer stretch of Amiantos to Kato Platres. After the phone conversation with Braun, Monir's mind was only minimally committed to the functions associated with driving. His body performed the movements automatically, but Monir's thoughts were nowhere near the road to Platres. He was inundated with fear and uncertainty. How could he possibly prepare for what was coming? How would he fare on Monday with Karl in the room?

As he pulled into a parking spot in the nearly empty car park at Pefkos Hotel, Monir felt one tiny ray of hope shining through the ominous cloud that had enveloped him: At least he knew what Karl was planning, and the CEO did seem to believe Monir would cooperate. *If anything, I may have just bought some time*, Monir thought optimistically.

He got out of the car and made his way to the front desk, oblivious to the black street bike slowly pulling into the car park behind him. The bike had been following Monir from Amiantos, maintaining a safe distance two to three cars back. Now it slowed to a stop next to Monir's car, its rider dismounting and leaning the bike on its kickstand. A black leather jumpsuit covered the rider's body; a helmet with a tinted face shield masked the rider's identity.

Lifting her face shield, Nadia scanned her surroundings for any sign of Monir. Seeing none, she took a small device from the storage area beneath the bike's seat. She knelt down as if to adjust something under the bike, then turned and reached under Monir's chassis, attaching the device to the car.

Less than thirty seconds after arriving, Nadia was back on the bike and on her way out of the car park. She rode to a clearing just up the road where, though several hundred meters away, she maintained a full view of the hotel's car park. She took off her helmet and pulled out a phone from her pocket. She dialed a long number and waited for a response.

"Is it done?"

"Yes. Everything is in place, Farrouk."

"Proceed as planned, then. Remember, set it off before he gets to a populated area. We can't risk the chance of any witnesses noticing you near the explosion."

She hung up and waited. It shouldn't be long before Monir reemerged from the hotel. *Sooner or later he'll be heading back down that mountain road toward his little girlfriend's place,* Nadia thought bitterly. *First Young, then the girl. Both of them die tonight.* She parked the bike in the shade and sat under a nearby pine tree, leaning back against it, eyes always focused on the Toyota in the hotel's car park.

She had closed her eyes for only a moment when she heard the crunching of gravel against the dirt. Footsteps. Nadia's eyes opened wide. She turned her head in the direction of the noise.

"Hiya. Beautiful up here, eh?" said a female hiker wearing an enormous backpack.

British, thought Nadia. Annoyed, she turned to the hotel for a quick look before responding to the intruder.

"Yes, this is a very nice area." She hoped her agreement would suffice and the stranger would keep on walking. No such luck.

The woman stopped a few feet from Nadia and tried to reach for something in her pack while still wearing it.

"I came up all the way from Trimiklini. The road gets very steep right around this spot. You taking a break from your bike? Where did you ride from?"

She kept switching arms to reach into the pouches of her backpack. Her mouth kept going as well.

"Trying to reach my water bottle. I'm afraid that if I take this pack off, I'll want to stop altogether. Do you mind helping me?"

Nadia looked at the woman incredulously, then walked over to her, maintaining a faint smile.

"Which side is it on?" she asked.

"Not sure. I think this one," the woman said, pointing to her right. The water bottle wasn't there. Nadia was frustrated and very uncomfortable, but there was no other way out of the awkwardness of the moment. She walked around the hiker and finally retrieved a water bottle from the other pouch.

"Here."

The woman thanked Nadia and drank from the bottle. "Much obliged, miss. Hope you have a splendid time on your ride."

Nadia nodded and returned to her spot by the tree. She kept an eye on the hiker until she was about 20 meters away, then she sat back down, her back against the pine. To Nadia's relief, nothing had changed in the car park. The Toyota was on the left, near the hotel's entrance.

The hiker walked a few hundred meters up the road, taking in the majestic view of the Platres Mountains. Turning back to look around, she nonchalantly reached into her pocket. She pressed a button on a small device and spoke, seemingly to the air.

"Do you copy?" she said, her British accent replaced by an American one.

"We copy, Cynthia. Loud and clear. Good job down there. We saw everything just fine."

"You like my performance, huh?"

"Yes, you deserve an Oscar." Laughter. "Your husband was successful as well."

"Oh, good. See you soon, then."

Cynthia Blake had distracted Nadia for only 23 seconds, but that was all the time Tyson Blake needed. In two hours, just as the sun would be making its final descent in the west, Monir would emerge from the hotel and enter his Toyota rental. He would drive out of the car park and take a right turn to head south toward Limassol. He would be followed from a distance by Nadia on her black street bike. On a straightaway before Moniatis, she would pull over, take out her phone, and tap in some numbers. Her gaze would be centered on Monir's car up ahead, waiting for it to be engulfed in flames, courtesy of the device she'd planted. Instead, she would hear the muffled sound of an explosion from the direction she had just come.

Tyson had buried the bomb shortly after retrieving it from the Toyota's chassis. Carrying it through the hotel's lobby in a black duffel bag, he'd jumped a small chain-link fence behind the hotel and walked across an alley to the car, where he reunited with his team. While Nadia was focusing her attention on the Toyota parked by the hotel's entrance, the bomb she had planted under the vehicle was being lowered into its final resting place deep in the Platres woods.

The team waited in the woods behind the hotel, keeping an eye on Nadia and Monir. Eventually the bomb went off, signifying two things. First, without the team's intervention, the CORE negotiator—a fellow American—would be dead. Second, Nadia and her people had failed, which wouldn't make them happy.

Still in her hiking gear, Cynthia rejoined Tyson and the others once Nadia had followed Monir up the road. "Glad to see you're all safe and sound," she said.

"You, too," Tyson said. "Nothing like jumping right into the action fresh from the airport, huh, Chandy?"

"Well, we do what we have to," Chandy said.

Cynthia finally unburdened herself from her backpack and put her arm around Tyson's waist. "How long did it take you guys to dig the hole?"

"Just a few minutes, no biggie," said Jeff Collins. "As long as Chandy made sure the Russian didn't detonate the bomb prematurely, we were fine. Another day in the office, if you ask me."

Cynthia rolled her eyes at Jeff. "I'm glad to see even an agency legend like yourself doesn't mind a little physical labor."

Nadia was dumbfounded by the bomb's outcome but could not go back to Kato Platres to investigate. She was forced to follow Monir all the way back to Amiantos, where she watched him park by the church courtyard and walk into the building through the side entrance. Stalo's car was already there.

The events of the next 48 hours would render Nadia and her accomplices incapable of finding out what happened to their explosive device. None of them would ever find out— and neither would the man whose life the bomb was intended to take.

Inside the church, Monir was greeted by Stalo and Father Mattheos. They sat down in wooden chairs the priest had set up in the back of the sanctuary. The holy man opened his palms, slightly extending his hands forward.

"Go ahead, my friend," he said in English, smiling at Monir.

Monir spoke with intentionality and conviction, pausing often for Stalo to translate. For the next new minutes, he gave Father Mattheos a quick overview of his assignment to secure a lithium contract for CORE. He also opened up to the man about discovering CORE's involvement in the murder of Davin Valois.

"The contract my company is hoping for is one that is written with innocent blood, and the deal—if it goes through—has the potential to destroy this country. I cannot let that happen, but I also don't know exactly how to proceed. Other than Stalo, you seem like the only person I can trust with this."

The priest was pondering what he had just heard. Monir continued, telling him how he stumbled upon Davin's name during his flight from Vienna.

"What's the chance, Father, that I hear that very same name again—this time in Cyprus? And from Stalo, the daughter of a total stranger who helped me after my car broke down in a ditch at the quarry?" Monir stopped to gauge how the priest was taking everything. "What I'm trying to say is…why me? There has to be a reason for all this. Where do I go from here? How do I solve this?"

Father Mattheos spoke, his tone loving, his eyes bright with excitement. Stalo translated, trying her best to capture and convey the holy man's demeanor.

"My dear friend, I don't know why you. But it is evident that you have been chosen to help this nation, to take a stand for our land and for our people. And Stalo was chosen to help you. So was I. So was the very land itself, and in these very mountains you are called to protect, I believe you'll find the answers."

"What do you mean?"

"The strategy you are seeking will come when you walk the land. Take a walk on the mountains, Monir, the higher up the mountain, the better." The priest pointed in the direction of Troodos. "Good things happen to our perspective when we take the high ground." He smiled and closed his eyes for a few moments.

Monir smiled broadly. He looked at Stalo, then back at the priest.

"I have to go. I know what to do."

He took the priest's hand with both of his and pressed it firmly between his palms.

"Thank you. Thank you!"

Monir exited the church, breaking into a run as he headed to his car.

Back inside the building, the holy man smiled at Stalo, seeing that she was debating whether to follow Monir. "Let him be," he said. "He got it, Stalo. He'll be OK."

Leaning back in his chair and turning his face toward the dome above, Father Mattheos closed his eyes again and whispered, "Thank you. Thank you!"

16

HUNTERS AND GATHERERS

Larnaca, Cyprus

Moscow had mandated that a phone meeting take place to assess the progress that Directorate S agents were making in blocking the lithium deal. Dimitry was happy to reconnect with his colleague, as the two of them went way back and had not spoken in months. Nadia only contacted her fellow Russian agents in Cyprus when necessary, to minimize the threat of detection.

"How are things, Dryovskaya? Looks like you have quite a juggling act on your hands."

"I'm fine. A bit challenging up in the mountains but nothing we can't handle."

"And how are your two agents faring?"

"I sent them back. After the Turks pulled out of the negotiations, there wasn't much to do around here. You seem to be handling the fronts very well."

"Any idea what the Americans are up to?"

"Nothing of substance. They're around, but they don't seem to be pushing for the deal. Who's asking?"

"I am. I think they got in our way yesterday, just like they did when I first got here back in March. CORE doesn't have the time to deal with them, but I thought maybe Moscow can help out."

Dimitry thought for a moment. "If they're not interested in the mineral, then their objective has to be similar to ours: keeping the others from getting it. But I do think their primary target is your Geneva employer. Either way, if other agencies are running interference on the deal, it means less work for you—as it pertains to your priorities with Moscow, that is. Right?"

"Yeah, except my boss in Switzerland gave me a specific assignment, and the Americans, or whoever else, may have gotten in the way."

"Ah, I see, we're on a mission to save face now, are we?"

"To hell with saving face! I need to do my job so that I can *do my job*, Dimitry. Get them off my back."

"I'll try to look into it for you. I'll be in touch."

*   *   *

Geneva

The call from Nadia came in at 3:30 AM, as expected. Karl answered after one ring.

"We still haven't found how he survived the bomb," Nadia said. "Someone intervened."

"And we don't have any time to keep digging, do we?"

"No, we don't. We have to deal with Young, first and foremost. Your subtle threats don't seem to have slowed him down, Karl. There is no way he can be at that meeting on Monday. Even with you present, he could wreck the deal and run for the hills."

"If he does, he won't be able to run far," Braun said, menace in his voice.

"Whoever bailed him out today would argue otherwise. But even if we did stop him from blowing the deal, it would be too late for us, wouldn't it?"

"If threats won't convince him, maybe something else will. Money has always worked before. Stock options? A seat at the table? Another holiday in the Alps? There has to be a way."

"I don't know, Karl. After meeting with the priest at the village, he went back to the hotel. Our people in Vienna intercepted an email Young sent to the Cyprus president's office requesting five minutes with him before the scheduled

217

meeting. He said he had evidence of foul play on every side of this deal."

"What do you recommend?"

"We still have eyes on his car. We find a way to take him out this weekend."

"And the meeting? What if the president asks about him? Wouldn't Monir's unexpected absence validate his allegations?"

"Your presence should take care of all that, Karl. You are CORE's CEO. Ultimately, Cyprus is dealing with you, not Monir Young. A few well-placed comments, along with your charm and persuasion, should facilitate the deal moving forward without another thought given to Young."

"So it's all on me at the meeting, then?"

"It's about time you earned your keep." She laughed loudly and said something in Russian. "What do you say, Karl?"

"Do it! No more surprises. And whatever you do, make sure they can't find a body. Not before Monday, anyway."

* * *

Kato Platres, Cyprus

There was something almost mystical about the way Father Mattheos had encouraged him to get alone in the mountains, Monir thought, and particularly about the way Monir had felt at that moment in the church. Whether there was a spiritual benefit from the holy man's advice was yet to be determined, but the change of scenery would undoubtedly help to recalibrate him.

Monir was desperate for a plan. He knew that his email to the president's office would have been intercepted by CORE, but he thought it might protect him from Karl, at least until the meeting. But then what? Even if he did manage to alert the president, how would he ever get off the island alive? Where could he go? And what about Stalo?

That priest may or may not have been inspired when he told me to head for Troodos, Monir thought, *but he was right about getting a high-ground perspective.*

A few days back, one of the young clerks at the village grocery store had told Monir about a good hiking trail. It was a dirt road that originated at Pano Platres, the village just above Kato Platres, and wound its way to the center of Troodos Village.

"It begins at a place called Psilo Thendro, which means 'tall tree,' just a few hundred meters in from the main

219

Platres-Troodos road," the clerk had said. "It's right near the president's summer residence. It's a beautiful trail that runs for about 13 kilometers. You will like it."

Monir woke with the sunrise. He lifted the shade in his room and looked at the mountains below. Another gorgeous summer morning. He dressed and had a quick breakfast of two eggs and toast topped with butter and fried halloumi cheese. He filled his backpack with the hiking essentials: water, a juice box, a few snacks, a small first-aid kit, an extra T-shirt, and a sweatshirt, just in case.

The 10-minute ride to the trail's starting point took Monir through the narrow streets of Kato Platres to the main road. He turned left and immediately noted the increase in the road's steepness. It was second and third gear for most of the remaining drive to Psilo Thendro.

The spot was easy to find, not just because of the massive eucalyptus rising above every other tree around it, but also because of the numerous red-plated rental cars parked in the tree's vicinity. The clearing and car park happened to be the starting point for one of the other famous trails in the area, Kaleidonia Falls.

Monir parked, grabbed his backpack, and locked the vehicle. He took a few moments to ensure he was at the right place and began to follow the dirt road marked with a small wood sign, "Troodos 13 km" burned into its center.

Staying a few hundred meters back from Monir's car, Dietrich and Yury followed him until he parked near the trail. They opened up a map of the area and quickly figured out that Monir was either hiking to the falls or to Troodos. They called Farrouk in Vienna.

"Looks like he's going hiking. We're not exactly sure which way he's heading, but we can figure it out."

"Perfect. Find him there. If at all possible, question him first. We need to find out who's been working with him. Shouldn't take long for him to crack."

The clerk was right. The trail Monir had taken offered spectacular views of mountains, valleys, and much of the island's southern coastline in the distant horizon. The vegetation along the trail was thick, and the rock formations on either side of the narrow road were imposing. Monir kept a steady pace and was not winded in the least, even while traversing the steep inclines along the way. His years of maintaining a consistent jogging regimen were paying off.

It was while he was fully engrossed in the sights around him that he heard the sound of an approaching vehicle. Monir turned around to see if he could spot the car on the road behind him. It took a few moments, but finally a white

SUV rounded the bend farthest from Monir's view. His heart started beating fast.

Could it be the white Lexus? he thought.

He rushed to a thicket nearby and hid until the car went past him. The vehicle was moving rather fast, but Monir was still able to make out the Lexus logo on the grill. He stayed crouched in the thicket until he could no longer hear the car, then rushed back to the trail. When he continued his ascent toward Troodos, Monir wasn't walking any longer. He was running.

Dietrich and Yury walked around Monir's car, looking for any signs that would point to Young's whereabouts. Within a few minutes they were tracing his footprints from the driver's door to the start of the dirt road. Looking up the trail, the two men recognized that rain had caused deep ruts in the dirt road, rendering it impassable for their Volkswagen Golf.

Yury called Nadia. "We need the Evoque in Platres. Immediately!"

"You should have thought of that earlier. I'm in the city. It'll take me an hour to get there."

"Just get here!"

Monir was getting winded, but he refused to stop running. He had to try and find the Lexus. He'd managed to catch a glimpse of a driver and someone sitting on the passenger's side. The back windows were tinted. *At least they didn't see me*, he thought.

Another car was coming up behind him. This time the bend in the road afforded no preview of it. Monir found a large boulder and ducked behind it. Another SUV roared past him. In spite of the thick cloud of dust the vehicle had kicked up, Monir could see the make and color. A green Mitsubishi.

It must be the Pajero, he thought. Monir waited for the car to round the next bend, then he took off running after it.

That's two—maybe the Range Rover will show up as well, he thought as he ran.

Nadia saw the Watchers from the main road and put on her turn signal. She put the car in park beside the wooden sign pointing to Troodos, got out, and walked to Dietrich, taking the Golf keys from his extended hand. Nadia told the men she'd head up to Troodos from the main road, then she'd enter the trail from the other end.

"That way Young will be trapped between us," she said.

Dietrich and Yury jumped in the Evoque and took off. By the time Nadia had started north with the Golf, her Range Rover was a hundred meters up the road, kicking up a sizable cloud of dust.

Dietrich was assessing the terrain while driving.

"Sheer rock faces on the left and steep drops on the right. There's no easy way off this trail."

"He's definitely up ahead," said Yury, "and he has no place to run. We'll find him or Nadia will. It's only a matter of time."

Monir was about eight kilometers along the trail when he saw a man standing atop a hill up ahead. Though the man was quite a distance away from him, Monir was still startled. Could he have been one of the passengers in the two vehicles that had gone by?

"C'mon up, friend. Wait till you see the view from here!" A slight echo of his voice bounced from a peak in the west. Obviously American. Southern accent.

Monir decided he had nothing to lose by climbing up to the man. At least he'd find out how the guy got there.

"OK. Just a minute." Monir scanned the slope for the easiest way up.

The man pointed down and to his right. "Right this way. That's how I came."

Monir followed a narrow, well-beaten trail and arrived at the top in a few minutes. He slowed down as he approached the man to get a better look at him.

"You're in great shape!" the man said. "I was winded halfway up this little molehill. Well done!"

Yury's phone buzzed. He picked up right away. "Not yet, but we are close."

The caller spoke a few sentences.

"Yes, Farrouk. I understand."

Dietrich turned to him the moment he hung up the phone. "What did he say?"

"Not to mess this up. Not to come back without results."

They looked at each other for a long moment. The German sped up. More dust.

"Jeff Collins," said the man with the Southern accent. His inviting smile and lively face complemented his firm handshake.

"Monir Young. Pleased to meet you. How did you—"

The man moved one step closer to Monir. His smile vanished, and his light brown eyes became intense.

"We don't have much time. I know this won't make any sense to you, but you will have to trust me. You are being pursued. Your life is in danger. I climbed up here to make sure they haven't caught up to you." He looked down the trail and paused for a listen.

"I don't think I follow," Monir said.

"Don't try to figure this out, Monir. Just listen to me. You need to go back down to the trail and keep walking toward Troodos. After the first bend in the road, you'll see the white Lexus that went by while you were hiding in that thicket. Make sure you get in it."

Monir looked beyond Collins for a moment and tried to formulate a response.

"Just go. Time is running out."

Monir found the white Lexus where Collins had told him it would be. The engine was idling. Drawing close to the vehicle from behind, Monir could see part of the driver's reflection in the side mirror. The man had his elbow out the window and was looking right at him. Monir approached the driver's window and awkwardly raised a hand in greeting. The man looked over his left shoulder to the back seat. The rear window came down halfway. A gray-haired man smiled at Monir.

"Hop in. Other side."

Monir walked around the car and reached for the handle. He saw a woman's eyes and blond hair in the passenger-side mirror. He opened the door and looked inside hesitantly.

"Come, come," said the man reassuringly. "We are Eli and Gina. Please, Mr. Young. We mean well. And don't worry about getting back to your car. We'll get someone to drive it up to us while we visit with you."

Monir consented. Maybe it was the peace in Eli's gray eyes or the soothing tone in his voice. Or maybe it was the good feeling he had about Jeff Collins that counted most. Somehow, he felt he could trust them.

Nadia arrived at Troodos Square, and after asking a shopkeeper for directions she took the first right turn for the trail. On the other end of the dirt road, the Evoque was stopping every few minutes. The Russian was checking for Monir's footprints. The arid terrain and thick, silty soil proved as accurate as any tracking device.

"He went that way," said Yury, pointing left. He had just assessed the ground in front of a fork in the road by Kaminaria. Seven or eight kilometers in that direction, they found the spot where Monir's feet seemed to veer off the road and up a ragged slope to the right, then back down toward Troodos.

But a second set of footsteps next to Monir's at the peak of the slope puzzled them. Yury was snapping pictures of the second set of footprints. Dietrich was yelling from below. Find Monir. Stick to the plan. With or without a companion, he had to be just up ahead.

"Mr. Young, you have inadvertently been implicated in a very dangerous scenario. Of greed. Of deception and avarice. Of murder. And of enormous geopolitical significance."

Eli and Gina shared a slight accent, but Monir had trouble placing it. Eli paused and took a reading of Monir's face. Before a question began to move from Monir's frowning forehead to his lips, Eli pressed on. "And your own life may be in danger."

"Who are you people?"

Gina spoke next. "Friends, Mr. Young, friends. Friends of Cyprus. Friends of justice. And your friends, if you wish."

Monir sat back and looked at the two of them. "Are your names really Eli and Gina?"

"Yes, of course," smiled Eli.

"Somehow I don't quite believe that," Monir said, smiling back.

They spoke for an hour in the living room of an old stone house on the western side of the mountain. Gina prepared coffee. The driver stayed with the car.

They had been watching him seemingly forever, and they seemed to know everything about him. Not just his activities surrounding CORE's pursuit of the lithium contract—everything. His Iranian mother, Suhir. Her flight from Tehran to the U.S. after the Shah was deposed. Her settling and education in America. Her meeting Derek Young at Georgetown Law School. Monir's upbringing in the suburbs of northern New Jersey. His first job as a delivery boy at Teaneck's Flower Shop. College grades, sports he played, license records with the DMV—anything with a paper trail connected to it seemed to be at Eli and Gina's disposal.

Then they started in on CORE. Again, they knew it all. Résumé details from his application for his position. His communications back and forth with his supervisors on the 32 projects he had undertaken in 14 nations over 23 years. His quarterly evaluations. Pay raises. Bank accounts. Addresses where he'd lived, contacts, phone numbers, habits—the works.

And, of course, everything that had happened in Cyprus. Including Stalo.

He didn't bother objecting to the invasion of privacy. Neither did he ask how they obtained the information. Somehow he knew that people who are capable of such feats don't share their secrets.

He'd once read a book about Israeli intelligence that a friend had given him. The more Eli and Gina talked, the more their accents—and their knowledge about him—convinced Monir that they were Israelis. When Eli and Gina had finished their tag team of know-and-tell, Monir calmly asked, "What made you go through, well, whatever it was you had to go through to learn so much about me?"

Eli took a sip of his coffee and looked out the window.

"You were given the assignment to negotiate on CORE's behalf. We would have been watching you regardless, just like everyone else who has been involved in this. Company protocol."

"You mean Israeli intelligence protocol?"

Eli ignored Monir's question and looked at Gina.

"It was your interesting ethnic background that sent us digging deeper than usual," Gina said. Her eyes met Monir's and held them without blinking.

"How so?"

"Our primary responsibility is to protect our people from our enemies, then to do our best to maintain peace in this part of the world. We have reason to believe CORE is connected to jihadist terrorism, and—" She cut herself off. Eli looked at her and held up his hand, motioning for her to slow down.

"CORE is not in Cyprus for the sole purpose of lining investors' pockets," Eli said. "There is a higher objective. For CORE, the stakes of this lithium deal are the resources to finance the operations of the relatively new, extremely violent breed of jihadist terrorists. You may have heard of them. They're called the Islamic State."

Monir's eyes went wide. "Wait a minute! CORE has ties to ISIS?"

It went back much further back and deeper than ISIS, Eli said. The Ottoman Empire's vast reach throughout Europe and the Middle East. The caliphate that operated from the Middle Ages until the start of World War I. The Ottoman belief that once a people were conquered, their nation was always under Ottoman rule. Cyprus had been overrun by the Ottomans in the eighteenth century. ISIS was among the numerous Islamic groups seeking to establish the long-awaited new caliphate that would have preeminence in the world. And ISIS leaders had ties to Karl Braun and CORE through Farrouk Ahmadi. "You know him, of course, Mr. Young?"

Monir was looking at the floor in a daze. "You can call me Monir," he said finally.

Eli continued. He explained how he and his colleagues had been tracing emails, phone calls, texts, encoded messages, and CORE profits from Swiss banks to places like Syria, Iraq, Yemen, and other hotbeds of ISIS activity. "We believed it was only a matter of time before you were pulled into all this, as either an accomplice or a victim." Eli paused to allow Monir to digest the information.

"Because…I'm Iranian?" Monir realized slowly.

"You're catching on quickly, Mr. Young—Monir," Gina said. "We had to dig deeper and watch closer, because we had to be sure."

"Sure of what?"

"That you would be willing to cooperate with us instead of them."

"And what makes you confident I'll do so?"

Eli tapped his temple and said, "You've been asking questions from here, because things didn't add up." He moved his palm to his chest. "But some answers have been coming from here, haven't they?"

Monir was speechless. He knew Eli hadn't reached that conclusion just by analyzing surveillance information. He bowed his head for a few seconds. Leaning forward, elbows on his knees, Monir placed his chin on his thumbs, the rest of his fingers interlocked in a praying posture.

"What would you like me to do?"

"First we have to make sure you stay safe. Listen carefully to Gina's instructions. Follow them closely. Now come, we'll take you back to your car. We'll be in touch soon."

Monir's car had been retrieved from Platres and driven to Troodos Square by two of Eli's people. The man who drove the Toyota parked it on the street, in front of a souvenir shop, then jumped in his colleague's car to return to the house. Without speaking a word, he delivered the keys to Eli's driver, who was waiting in the Lexus.

When Eli's SUV pulled up to the Toyota, Monir turned to Eli with a question. "Why did they park it here instead of your house?"

"Again, Mr. Young, we have reason to believe you are being watched. We had to take every precaution to ensure that your pursuers don't find us in the process."

By the time Monir left Eli and Gina, the Watchers were having coffees at a roadside kiosk in Korfi, halfway between Troodos and Limassol. They'd found the last of Monir's footprints by the tracks of a large vehicle—obviously, Monir's hike had given way to a drive. Shortly afterward, Nadia arrived in the Golf, coming from the other direction.

"Anything?" she asked Yury.

"He must have been picked up by someone right around here."

"Damn it! It must have been the white SUV that went by me just as I was turning for the trail."

She turned around and followed the SUV's tread marks to the center of Troodos, where dirt finally met asphalt in front of a three-way turn. The three Watchers looked left, down the mountain, then right, toward Troodos Square. They chose left. The chase was off.

Monir shut the Lexus door and walked to his car. Turning around one last time before entering the vehicle, he attempted an awkward wave goodbye. Eli waved back, but his hand and face quickly gave way to Monir's own reflection as the tinted window slid closed. The white SUV pulled away slowly. Monir sat in his car, closed his eyes, and exhaled. It felt as though he'd been holding that breath for days, maybe even months.

17

EXECUTE!

Limassol, Cyprus

Everyone at CORE was livid that Monir had escaped from the Watchers' traps twice. Undoubtedly, he'd had help, and that would have to be taken into consideration in the next—and hopefully last—attempt against him. There was no more room for failure. Farrouk told Braun and Nadia that he was sending in Khalid so that CORE would finally have someone competent in Cyprus.

Nadia and her fellow Watchers met Khalid at the Amadonia Beach Hotel. Khalid, Dietrich, and Yury sat in armchairs while Nadia stood beside the large dining room table and walked them through her plan. Monir's attachment to the local Amiantos woman rendered him impermeable to seduction. But to her knowledge, and that of her teammates, neither Monir nor Stalo had ever laid eyes on any of them. That meant the Watchers could get near them at a public place and carry out a swift offensive.

"Shock and awe," she said. "When we find them, I'll make my move, which will ensure they leave quickly, and, most importantly, separately. Khalid stays in the Evoque. I join him once the girl leaves, and we trail her. Yury and Dietrich, you follow Monir. Farrouk said to call him before you strike."

She directed their attention to a large map that had been laid out on the table.

"Monir will be heading….here," Khalid said. He'd been studying the Limassol–Troodos route on and off since he had arrived from Vienna. His eyes stayed on the map as his finger wove its way south-to-north along the main road. "Platres, right?"

"Yes, his hotel is there."

Khalid continued. "And the girl has to take this right turn at…Sa-e-ttas. That seems to be the only way to her little village, yes?"

"Saittas," Nadia offered. "Benefit of having been on this island for way too long," she said coldly.

"Good, then. Dietrich and Yury, you take him here." Khalid backed up his finger to about the central point on the route. "Just after the dam."

"Good spot," said Nadia. "Road gets steeper, with many bends along the way. Huge drops on the left, too, in case we need to dump the body quickly. They'll never find him there."

Khalid turned to Nadia and moved his finger accordingly.

"And you and I hit her here at the halfway point between the Saittas turn toward Amiantos and the village. As long as they leave separately, we should have no problems."

"We are certain that they will be arriving at the restaurant separately, and I will make sure they leave separately as well."

"Two birds with two stones," Khalid said, smirking. Nadia smiled for half a second, then reverted to steely-eyed seriousness.

Recent surveillance by the Watchers had indicated that on Sunday evening Stalo and Monir planned to attend an event for Stalo's company at Oasis Bar and Grille, a popular hangout in the western outskirts of Limassol. A few emails and phone conversations pointed to a small gathering of Stalo's coworkers and employers to celebrate someone's upcoming retirement. Stalo saw the function as an opportunity to introduce Monir to everyone.

Stalo was also one of the organizers of the celebration. According to the plans she and Monir had made earlier in the week, she would head to the city early in the afternoon to help one of her coworkers put together a small presentation for the retiree. Monir would drive down by himself a few hours later to join her at the restaurant.

In spite of all the upheaval of the last few days, the Watchers believed Stalo and Monir would still attend the event because of the professional component for Stalo. She wouldn't stand up her coworkers, they guessed, especially since she was one of the organizers. The Watchers were proven correct.

Knowing he and Stalo might be a target at the event, and knowing the event was important to Stalo, Monir asked Eli and Gina for their help. The Israelis hadn't had time to bug Khalid's suite, due to the Syrian's sudden arrival. Even so, Eli's instincts led him to prepare for several possible scenarios. Gina called Monir and Stalo on Saturday night to give them instructions. She texted the couple pictures of Nadia, Dietrich, and Yury—they didn't yet have one of Khalid.

Something about Nadia seemed familiar to Monir, but he couldn't quite place her. He stared at the picture, willing himself to remember where he'd seen her, but nothing was coming to mind. She was an attractive woman; maybe she just reminded him of other attractive women he'd seen. He decided not to mention it to Eli and Gina.

"If you see any of them, contact us immediately," Gina said. "Whatever you do, do not leave the restaurant unless we tell you it is safe."

Oasis on Sunday night was packed. All the tables were full, as were the bar stools. Even the few benches by the walls, intended to be decorative, had couples sitting on them.

Monir and Stalo were barely able to hear each other over the loud music. The retirement ceremony, and the introductions of Monir to Stalo's coworkers, had taken place earlier, before the Sunday night crowd arrived. Though everyone was seated at a long table, the noise was making mingling and conversation difficult. After a few failed attempts to talk, Monir and Stalo settled for sipping their drinks and watching the crowd around them. Stalo was trying to act normal among her colleagues, but Monir's eyes were scanning the crowd for the Watchers Gina had shown them.

Suddenly, he saw her—the woman from the pictures. Not just the ones from Gina, but also, he now remembered, the ones he himself had taken of that same woman in Geneva's airport in January. Blond hair, a colorful scarf, and black boots. Monir avoided eye contact with the woman and discretely pulled out his phone. He had to make sure. Stalo was taking a sip of her Margarita while waving at some of her friends on the dance floor. She was unaware of the woman or that Monir's trembling index finger was actually searching for the photo file he had titled "Davin Valois" after his flight. He found the photos. It was her.

Remembering his instructions from Gina, Monir began to type on his phone. First he would text her a 10-digit numeric code to identify himself, then he would send a coded message. He didn't make it far. Out of the corner of his eye he saw the woman moving toward their table. When he looked up, the woman's eyes were fastened on his as she closed the distance between them. Stalo saw the look on Monir's face and followed it to the woman, who was walking past her at that very moment.

Slowly and purposefully, Nadia walked right up to Monir and took hold of his arm. Instinctively, he stood up to pull away from her, but Nadia tightened her grip and pulled him even closer. Though her hand was applying strong pressure on Monir's bicep, Nadia's smiling face and playfully tilted head were communicating something completely different. Stalo was on her feet as well, a confused expression on her face.

"Hello, darling," Nadia shouted at Monir over the music. She looked at Stalo. "Is this the little Cypriot girl you were telling me about? You were right—she is cute, for a local."

Before Monir could react, Nadia reached behind Monir's head, took hold of his hair, and pulled his face into hers. She connected with his lips and kissed him passionately. He tried to wrench himself free, but the shock of the moment, as well as her grip on his arm and head, had a stunning effect. Stalo was frozen in her seat, completely helpless.

The kiss lasted a few seconds, but it felt like an eternity to Monir. Then Nadia, with a broad smile still on her face, ran her hand down his cheek and neck. She leaned into his ear and said, "Good to be with you again." The music made it impossible for anyone else to hear her, but the familiarity she projected throughout the entire exchange did the trick.

Monir looked at Stalo, whose eyes were full of tears and whose hand was reaching for her purse. She gave him one last look of anger and despair, then she stormed out the door. His cry of "Wait!" was muffled by the music blasting through the speakers.

He tried to move toward the door, only to be stopped by another death grip, this time on his forearm. "Don't," Nadia said. The smile and head tilt were long gone. She pushed Monir forcefully to the floor, then reached over to snatch his phone from the table. As Stalo's coworkers looked on, bewildered, Nadia slipped out of the restaurant. She was beside Khalid in the Evoque in seconds.

In the eyes of anyone who saw the incident, it looked like nothing but relationship-related drama—so much so that some of Stalo's male colleagues hesitated to help Monir up off the floor. The commotion continued for a few minutes, delaying Monir from exiting the restaurant. By the time he ran out into the car park, there was no sign of Stalo anywhere. The spot her car had occupied, right next to his, was empty. And the woman who had assaulted him was nowhere to be found.

Monir's Toyota shot out of the car park, exiting the Marina area and turning left toward the port. He followed the road toward My Mall, Limassol's largest shopping establishment, intending to head back north through a backroad shortcut Stalo had shown him a few days prior.

Yury and Dietrich followed him, maintaining a hundred-meter buffer from the Toyota. The two men remained quiet, their eyes fastened on Monir's taillights.

Khalid had gone over the plan in detail once more before they left the hotel. "Pass him, speed ahead of him, and then block the road. Pretend you broke down and need help. When he stops, shoot him. You have to do all this very quickly because of oncoming traffic. If time permits, load the body in his trunk; if not, dump him over the cliff and drive his car back to the hotel. We'll hide it later, when we all get back together." Khalid and Nadia would follow a similar plan for Stalo.

Monir crossed the bridge by Kouris Dam and started up the mountain. On the second sharp turn, he had to slow down significantly. Just a few meters ahead was a garbage truck, manifesting the usual struggle that diesel engines have on steep roads. According to Stalo's impeccable—though oddly detailed—knowledge of the garbage truck schedule, as well as Monir's own miserable experience a few nights earlier, the truck's presence on the road didn't make sense. It was not garbage collection day, and even if it was, the truck was out at least two hours early. And where were the other six or seven trucks that usually constituted the trash-collection convoy?

Monir passed the truck on the next short straightaway. His pursuers were behind it next, but they never had the opportunity to pass. As soon as Monir had rounded the next bend, the truck suddenly swerved to the right, blocking both lanes. While idling in that diagonal position, the driver and a passenger jumped down from the vehicle and made their way to the back.

To the frustrated Watchers, the two men seemed to be shifting around the garbage bags. Yury was on the phone with Farrouk. Victor was busy laying on the horn. Neither was prepared for the two men to pull out .45s with suppressors. Four bullet holes appeared in the car's windshield as two bullets struck each Watcher, one in the head, one in the chest. The blaring horn worked in the garbage men's favor, further muffling the shots. The two men kept their weapons leveled at the car as they quickly approached it to check on the Watchers. No other shots were fired. None were needed.

On either side of the incident, a white Lexus and a green Pajero blocked traffic in both directions. Four red flares were set in the middle of the road. The SUVs' drivers informed the handful of stopped motorists of the cause for the delay. "There was an accident. Should be cleaned up in no time."

It was. And when traffic resumed on the Limassol– Troodos road a few minutes later, nothing was seen at the site of the "accident" by drivers from either direction.

The shooters had carried the bodies to the garbage truck and disposed of them. Then one of the men drove the truck down the mountain while the other followed in the Watchers' car. No one would ever see the rental, or the bodies, again.

Near Saittas, the second garbage truck, similarly manned and equipped, pulled in front of Stalo's VW out of the Tjunction that led to Pelendri and Agros. Khalid and Nadia were in the red Range Rover, a few hundred meters behind Stalo. The truck driver kept the two cars behind him in his sights as he made the right turn for Amiantos. As in the case of the Limassol–Troodos road, passing would be very difficult from that point on. On a short straightaway, the truck veered over to the left, almost scraping against the rocky embankment, allowing Stalo to pass. Before the Evoque could follow, the truck moved back to the right, fully occupying the left lane of the road. Four kilometers up, it sped to the next sharp turn to further distance itself from the Range Rover. By the time Khalid rounded the same turn, the garbage truck had already blocked the road. The driver and passenger were jumping to the ground. The Evoque screeched to a halt.

The police report about the "Garbage Truck Incident," as it would later be referred to by locals, would state that two different farmers heard shots around midnight. One testified to three shots; the other said he heard more. The two men found lying by the back of the truck were wearing garbage collectors' uniforms. Both had one bullet wound in the forehead. Both of them looked Mediterranean, but it was clear they were not Cypriots. A third man, later identified by his Syrian passport as Khalid Homsi, was found dead on the side of the road. A Beretta handgun was recovered two feet away from him. Evidence pointed to a lethal shootout between him and the other victims.

Rumors spread that a week after the incident a diplomatic delegation from Israel was sent to Cyprus to escort the two unidentified bodies to Tel Aviv. One Amiantos man, whose brother worked at the airport, said that a gray-haired man and a blonde woman were seen standing silently by the coffins of the two men until they were loaded onto the private jet that had brought the officials from Israel. Then everyone boarded and the plane took off.

18

THE TRADE

Monir and Stalo did not find out about the garbage truck shootings until the next day. With Monir's phone in the hands of Nadia, and Stalo heartbroken by the incident at Oasis the night before, the couple would not communicate at all before Monir's meeting in Nicosia. Monir was desperate to explain Nadia's cruel trick to Stalo, but for now his focus had to be on the Monday meeting with the president and Cypriot officials.

Gina was waiting for Monir in the lobby of his hotel when he arrived there late Sunday night. She escorted him to his room, where she assured him that her people were taking care of things pertaining to the scene at the restaurant earlier. She said nothing about the operation that had saved his and Stalo's lives that night.

"Everything will work out, Monir. And I'll explain things to Stalo. Trust me. Now, we need to talk about tomorrow."

Gina laid it out plainly. Monir's part was simply to follow Karl's orders to book a limo for airport pick-up. Inform his boss through an email that everything was in place, then head to the Hilton in Nicosia for the meeting.

"As for what you say during the meeting, Monir, remember what we discussed up at Troodos. And never any mention of our association, of course."

The limo service Monir had arranged met Karl in the arrivals hall at the airport. The driver, a pleasant man of medium build, greeted his passenger after Braun acknowledged his pick-up sign with a nod.

"I'm Panos. At your service, sir." He helped Karl with his carry-on bag and escorted him to the car park.

With a warm smile, Panos opened the rear passenger-side door of the black Lincoln. He pointed to the small drink rack built into the door paneling and offered Karl refreshments. "Anything you want, sir. Make yourself comfortable." He spoke English with a characteristic thick Greek accent, rolling all his r's. Soft drinks, small water bottles, a couple of Smirnoff vodka coolers, and an unopened bottle of Johnny Walker Black Label were the options. Karl reached over, pulled out one of the water bottles, and twisted off the cap.

Within minutes, the limo had cleared the airport area and began the 35-minute northward journey to the capital. It would be mostly highway with no traffic, a straight shot to Nicosia. Braun was hoping he might even have time to take a shower before the eleven o'clock meeting.

Twenty kilometers before reaching his passenger's destination, the driver took the exit toward the village of Tseri. Turning right at the end of the exit ramp and following the road toward the limestone hills surrounding the village, Panos turned right onto a dirt road and continued for two kilometers. The Lincoln then took a left onto a narrower dirt road. The driver pulled out a radio. "Heading your way. Two minutes out." His English with a Greek accent had given way to Hebrew.

Karl did not take note of the language switch. He did not protest the diversion from the highway, nor did he complain about the bumpy off-road trek. The German was bent over, head bumping against the passenger seat, body jerking involuntarily as the Lincoln rambled along the dips and potholes.

At Karl's feet lay the small water bottle, most of its contents spilled onto the carpeted maroon floor mat. Only one sip had been ingested from the bottle. But since one gram of polonium-210 can kill easily, one sip was more than enough to eliminate the CEO.

The president's motorcade, comprising the presidential Mercedes Benz, three black BMWs, and several police motorcycles, arrived at the Hilton promptly at 11:00 AM. The president, escorted by two aides, the chief of police, and a number of bodyguards, walked briskly to the conference room, where Monir Young was sitting on a sofa. Three policemen and two plainclothes guards who had arrived earlier to secure the room stood near him.

Chief of Staff Costas Eleftheriou, Department of Mining head Orestis Sophroniou, Cyprus Sovereign Bank manager Giannis Theodorou, and mining official Angelos Mavros were not present in the room. Each of them had been arrested by Criminal Investigation Department officers earlier that morning and had been transported to Nicosia's police headquarters for questioning.

The arrests were made after a thumb drive was delivered to the chief of police by a U.S. embassy courier just before midnight on Sunday. The drive contained unquestionable evidence—dozens of emails and several recordings of phone conversations—proving that the four Cypriot men had conspired with CORE's CEO and at least three CORE employees to manipulate the Cypriot government for acquisition of the lithium rights. A note accompanied the thumb drive, stating that CORE negotiator Monir Young, along with Amiantos resident Stalo Leontiou, both of whom were not implicated in the injunctions, had further information regarding the conspiracy as well as CORE's involvement in the murder of Davin Valois in Vienna.

The president and his entourage walked briskly into the conference room and turned to Monir, who stood to greet them. Cyprus's leader shook Monir's hand as he introduced himself with his first name. He then waved off most of the others in the room, retaining only the chief of police and one bodyguard.

The president asked Monir to sit by him at the long conference table. The other two men remained standing.

"Mr. Young, on behalf of a grateful nation, I personally thank you for everything you have done, and will continue to do, I'm sure, to shed light on the crimes of CORE and some of our own citizens."

The president had the police chief inform Monir that he was being summoned to police headquarters for testimony immediately after the meeting. Stalo Leontiou had already been notified and would meet him there.

Then the president asked his two men to leave the room. Once they had, he continued.

"Mr. Young, when I was elected two years ago, I vowed that I would do my best to eradicate corruption from this government. Today's arrests, in large part due to your assistance in this whole matter, are a milestone for us. Thank you."

"I'm honored to be of help to you and your people, Mr. President," Monir said.

"You've traveled the world, you've seen many things, Monir—may I call you by your first name?"

Monir nodded.

"You have connections with many leaders, governments, and the like. And now, of course, you've had an insider's perspective of the lithium find here in Cyprus. Do you have any insights for us pertaining to the lithium rights?"

"I do, Mr. President," Monir said. "Your comment about eradicating corruption reminds me of when I was pursuing mining contracts in Asian markets. I became acquainted with several members of Singapore's government. That nation, especially under the leadership of the late Mr. Lee Kuan Yew—perhaps you know of him—"

"I do—it was, in fact, his leadership model that first inspired me to pursue a corruption-free course."

"Well, Singapore is on the rise—has been for quite some time now—and I believe it is likely to be interested in partnering with Cyprus for the lithium. Moreover, I would recommend your Middle Eastern neighbors Israel."

The president chuckled and looked thoughtful for a moment. "I suppose we had better do that. Something tells me they had a hand in what transpired here today." He looked at Monir for a reaction that might verify his statement.

Monir simply smiled and continued. "I believe they can be trusted to have your best interests at heart."

The president stood and offered his hand. "Mr. Young, after everything is finished—your statement for the police, the sorting out of the matters surrounding this whole situation—would you consider further discussing the possibility of working with us, even in those very nations you mentioned, for the lithium deal?"

Monir stood too and shook the president's hand. "Of course, Mr. President. Looks like I'll be in need of a new job anyway." Both men laughed.

"Take good care of yourself, Monir. We'll talk soon."

"Thank you, Mr. President."

Monir met Stalo at CID headquarters in Nicosia. She glared at him the moment he walked through the door. The officer at the front desk stepped outside to give the two a moment.

Stalo stood up. Monir walked right to her and wrapped his arms around her shoulders. She took a deep breath and then composed herself to speak.

"Gina came over last night, after she left your hotel. She explained everything. She said they're still looking for the woman, who was most likely Davin's killer. I'm so sorry that I mistrusted you, Monir. It just hit me so—"

"I'm falling for you, Stalo Leontiou." Monir held her for a moment longer, then let her go so he could look into her eyes. "As far as I'm concerned, all the good that's coming out of this whole thing is because of you. And we're just getting started."

They embraced again, remaining that way until a faint knock on the door signaled the deputy's return.

Outside the U.S. embassy the next morning, the green Pajero led the way, submitting the appropriate paperwork at the outer guard post. The officer looked everything over and opened the gate. The Pajero and the Lexus behind it entered the embassy courtyard and parked. The Lexus's driver stayed with the car while its two passengers, Eli and Gina, accompanied Chandy, Jeff, Tyson, and Cynthia into the embassy.

The six of them met briefly with the U.S. ambassador, who expressed thanks for their cooperation as well as his heartfelt condolences for the loss of Eli and Gina's two colleagues.

Then the agents convened in the small room that had been assigned to Tyson and Cynthia Blake as an office. Over coffee and cookies, they talked things over.

Tyson was stirring a packet of sugar into his coffee when he asked, "What's the word on CORE?"

"Their Cyprus funds have been frozen and will probably be seized, pending trial, of course. Executives will probably avoid incrimination, and the company will stay in business, but it'll never be the same without Braun," replied Eli.

"I heard he mysteriously disappeared shortly after his arrival on the island," offered Cynthia with a wink at Gina. "Plus, they lost Young, who may be offering his consulting services to the Cypriot government in the days ahead."

Several smiles and chuckles, then Eli asked, "And the Russian? Where do you think she is?"

"She either left already or she's on her way out. We're watching the airports in Larnaca and Paphos. But I don't think we'll have any luck apprehending her."

Chandy spoke up. "People like her have a way of slipping through the cracks, don't they?"

"Only to reemerge at another place and time," said Tyson. "She'll be back soon enough, and we'll get her—or you guys will. It's just a matter of time. "

Monir had made the reservation on his way back from the capital. The four of them—Father Mattheos and his wife, Stalo, and Monir himself—would meet at Katoi Restaurant around noon the next day. Monir had arranged for the lunch primarily to honor the priest for his input a few days back, but for another reason as well.

As promised by Stalo, Katoi was exceptional. In both cuisine and décor, the restaurant offered a perfect blend of traditional and modern. Beyond its chef's talent and creativity with culinary delicacies, the restaurant was owned by a most hospitable and friendly couple who always made it a point to visit every table to greet their customers.

"I hope your meal was enjoyable," Monir said to the priest and his wife, smiling and pointing to their nearly empty plates. The couple needed no translation.

"Very good, thank you," responded the priest in English.

The table was cleared and coffee was served.

"On the house," offered Katoi's owners.

Monir then asked the question that had been burning in him over the last couple days.

"Father, I'm increasingly aware—Stalo and I, that is—we know that some people have collaborated to make sure that we stayed safe, and that we did what was best for Cyprus."

The priest nodded thoughtfully. His contemplative frown signified that he had heard Monir's statement but was not confirming it.

"Your suggestion to go out to the land and, in a sense, let it speak to me—was that part of my mystery allies' plan?"

The priest listened to the translation and turned toward his wife. She smiled and shook her head. The priest grinned at first, then he chuckled.

"I'm happy to know you had help, Monir, because as things turned out, you really needed it!"

Everyone laughed.

"But what I said to you back at the church did not come from your allies here in Cyprus. That advice, that help, did not come from here," he said, moving his palm downward toward the stone tiles. "It came from—" The priest kept his eyes on Monir and pointed his right index finger upward.

Monir wanted to ask a follow-up question but couldn't find the words. Father Mattheos's blue eyes were smiling. Monir looked at Stalo. Tears were forming in her eyes. The clergyman grinned and shrugged. He reached over and placed his hand on Monir's shoulder.

"You understand, my friend?"

Monir fought back tears of his own. "Yes...yes, I understand."

The immigration officer at the Larnaca airport took a quick glance at the woman in front of him while scanning her passport. Her straight red hair curved inward with perfect symmetry, just below her cheeks. Her sparkling green eyes were looking beyond the officer toward the checkpoint. Her feigned indifference allowed him to steal an extra second or two to admire her beauty. She looked back at him and smiled. His cheeks flushed. The scan now complete, the officer stamped the passport and smiled.

"Have a safe flight, Ms. Dryovskaya."

After clearing security, Nadia walked past the duty-free shops and restrooms, taking a right turn toward the sitting area in front of Gate 46. The area was completely deserted, as the next flight was hours away. She walked to the last row of empty seats in front of the gate and took a seat facing the windows. During the next few minutes she placed two phone calls. The first was to Vienna.

"How did you know to alert me, Farrouk?"

"I was on the phone with Yury when they got ambushed. He'd been updating me as they were about to make their move on Young. I heard Dietrich swearing at a truck that was blocking his way. Then I heard gunshots and I lost them."

"Thanks for the heads-up. I owe you my life."

"Don't mention it. Where are you going next?"

"Vienna. It's why I'm calling. I have something for you, Farrouk. Can we meet briefly?"

"Of course. The usual place?"

"Yes, the riverside car park across from the opera house is fine. I'll look for your car around nine o'clock. See you there."

Nadia pulled a second secure phone out of her purse and dialed a 16-digit number. At the prompt, she entered eight more digits. Then she spoke her last name.

A short pause, a click as though the call had been dropped, and then a deep male voice.

"You OK? Picked up chatter about some shootings."

"Yes, I'm fine, thanks to the Jordanian. It was—"

"Israelis, the boss says. And he's already deployed a team to sort this out—on their soil. You coming in?"

"Yes, after a quick detour."

"Where?"

"Vienna."

"What for?"

"Tying up loose ends."

"Understood. Be careful. See you soon."

Nadia looked down at her watch. Just under an hour before OS 831 would be boarding at Gate 32 for Vienna. She took her time walking through the stores and browsing perfumes and face lotions. She meandered toward the wine section and reached for a bottle of Vlasides Shiraz from the shelf. She looked at it and half-smirked.

Great wine! Helped take down the Frenchman, and now it's the Jordanian's turn, she thought.

While walking to the checkout counter, she played the scenario in her head.

With my heartfelt thanks, Farrouk. It's the best of Cyprus.

Wine bottle in hand, Farrouk would look down at the label for two seconds, maybe three. Her left hand would have already slipped under the wide pant leg of her jeans to pull out the black tactical blade from the sheath strapped on her ankle. One swift, fluid motion would follow, and the Jordanian ISIS fundraiser would be clutching his throat. Blood would begin to cover his fingers. Two large black eyes would be staring at her in disbelief, but not for long. In just a few moments they would close forever.

Sorry, Farrouk, but Moscow doesn't want any survivors.

Nadia pulled out a 50-euro bill and paid for the wine. Then she headed for her gate. Narrowing her eyes and pursing her lips, she hissed a threat to some empty seats up ahead. Then in Russian she said, "I'm coming for you too, Monir Young. You and your precious girlfriend. Sooner or later, however long it takes. I will find you, and I will kill you."

EPILOGUE

Larnaca, Cyprus

The plane lifted off at 7:55 PM, as scheduled. After the landing gear retracted and the aircraft performed a 180-degree turn over Larnaca's harbor, BA 220 climbed steadily toward the western horizon. The skies were spotless and deep blue. Within 10 minutes of takeoff the right wing tipped slightly and the plane headed northwest, toward the western edge of the Troodos Range. From his window seat, Monir looked down at the rocky, pine-covered mountains. The last rays of the setting sun were highlighting entire slopes, along with the numerous small communities tucked between the terrain's nooks and folds.

Every village and town would have peace that night, and for many nights to come. No one would be recklessly digging around them for lithium; no one would be exploiting the people for monetary gain. And no emerging or self-proclaimed caliphate would be funded on Cyprus soil.

"I will not forget you, Troodos," Monir said softly. "I'll be back. We'll both be back, soon."

He turned his face to the left, realizing that the beautiful woman sitting next to him had heard him. Stalo looked into Monir's eyes, moved her right hand across the tray table between them, and laid it on his forearm. She squeezed gently, smiled, and nodded.

"We will. We will."

AUTHOR'S NOTE

The Trade is a work of fiction, written for entertainment. The names, characters, places, and incidents portrayed in the story are either imaginary or have been used fictitiously. Any resemblance to actual persons living or dead, businesses, companies, governments, events, or locales is entirely coincidental.

There is, indeed, an old defunct quarry just north of the village of Amiantos; however, lithium is yet to be found there. The village of Amiantos also exists, and some farmers still ride donkeys to their fields. Geological teams from Europe and the U.S. visit Cyprus regularly to explore the island's unique and diverse rock formations.

Many of the restaurant and hotel names are fictitious, but I left some unchanged. Makris Family Restaurant in Platres, for instance, is a personal favorite—my wife and I have always enjoyed their lamb chops. Similarly, Katoi in Omodos is an outstanding restaurant whose chef and owners embody everything that is wonderful about Cypriot hospitality. We are fortunate to consider them friends. Vlasides wine is among the finest in the land, and the Shiraz is truly

263

outstanding. Many other Cypriot wineries are increasingly producing remarkable wines. One of the country's greatest gifts to locals and tourists alike is the food and drink produced there, as well as the amazing hospitality of the people who serve it in their homes and restaurants.

I apologize to every establishment, in Cyprus and abroad, where I proposed that the book's shady characters conducted their meetings. Vienna and Geneva are among my favorite cities in the world, and I believe they wouldn't have tolerated the evil perpetrated by CORE's leaders and employees.

It is highly unlikely that an Iranian American like Monir Young would work closely with and represent Cyprus's government, particularly the president. But I believe my portrayal of the need for foreign professional input into Cypriot geopolitics is genuine. A president who is fully committed to a corruption-free administration has yet to arise in Cyprus, but the inspiring story of Singapore—an island city-state that emerged from poverty to great prowess in one generation—offers a model that can positively affect Cyprus's future.

There is a Cafe Anamnisis in Cyprus, but it is not located next to the demarcation line by the old city walls of Nicosia. Yet my description of the militarized border is accurate. Many Cypriot soldiers have stood at guard posts all across the divided capital with a view of their families' pre-1974 properties on the Turkish-occupied side. In spite of countless attempts by both sides to solve "The Cyprus Problem" over the last 40 years, at the time this book went to print, no viable solution had yet been reached.

The church at Amiantos is not led by Father Mattheos; however, the island is richly blessed by many insightful and sincere clergymen like him. I take this opportunity to honor the Greek Orthodox Church for peacefully and faithfully maintaining a strong Christian witness in the region, in spite of many trials and persecutions in seasons past and present.

I doubt that any of the American Academy's graduates came from Amiantos village; however, I opted for that detail in Stalo's life to honor my high school for establishing strong foundations in academics and character for more than 100 years.

I began to write *The Trade* primarily because of encouragement I received from my two sons and some good friends from Georgia and North Carolina. Thank you, guys—I hope you were right.

My childhood friend Antonis—a successful Cypriot entrepreneur and owner of several quarries—lent his expertise in the area of drilling and blasting methods. Many thanks!

I salute the remarkable team of professionals who helped with production. Mark DeJesus (formatting and consultation); Sergio Barrera (cover and website design); and JM Olejarz (editing of the manuscript). I appreciate them for being so pleasant to work with and for insisting on excellence. We worked diligently to rid the manuscript of typos and syntax, grammar, and formatting bugs, but some may have eluded our eyes. I take full responsibility for them.

Lastly, I honor my wife and children for their patience and sacrifice throughout the duration of this yearlong project. I wholeheartedly dedicate this book to them.

Trace Evans is the pen name of an author who has published several inspirational books. Drawing from his international background, elite military training, and extensive travels, Trace makes his fiction debut with a riveting plot set in one of the most turbulent regions of our planet. Trace is of Greek-Cypriot descent and now resides in the northeastern United States with his wife and three children.

You may contact Trace Evans at www.traceevans.com or author.traceevans@gmail.com.

Thank you for your purchase of *The Trade*!

Made in the USA
Charleston, SC
13 December 2016